A DISBELIEF IN DEMIGODS

A DISBELIEF IN DEMIGODS

Stephen Measure

silverlayer.com

Silver Layer Publications
P.O. Box 1047
Chino Valley, AZ 86323

Paperback ISBN: 978-1-940778-53-2
Ebook ISBN: 978-1-940778-52-5

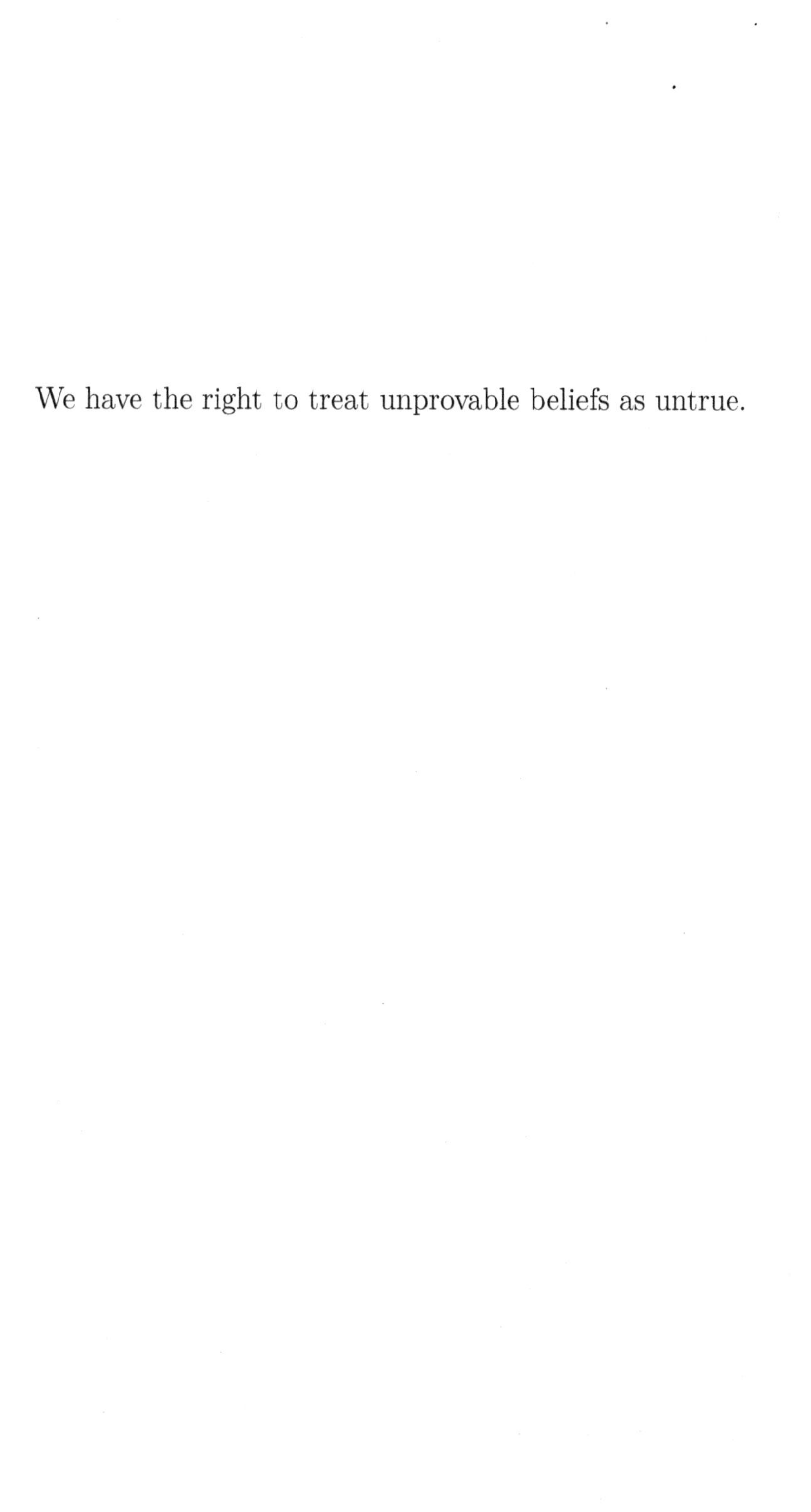

We have the right to treat unprovable beliefs as untrue.

Contents

The Coming Out	1
The Freedom to Not Believe	9
Gender Identity and the Invisible Pasta God	17
There Can Be No Demigods in Secularism	71
Unwanted Proof	79
It's Gender-Obscuring, Not Gender-Affirming	119
A Principal's Conundrum	123
'What Is a Woman?' Answered	129
The Psychologist	135
Provable Reality, Cold and Indifferent	151
Converting the Two-Spirit	153
There Is No Valid Proof of Gender Identity ...	163
Appendix: Original Publication Dates	187

The Coming Out

"Mom, we need to talk," Meghan said and she sat down at the kitchen table, facing her mother.

"Is it about your rainbow-colored ponytail?" her mother said, closing her cookbook and looking up at Meghan. "Yes, it does make you look ridiculous."

"What?" Meghan said, pulling her ponytail over her shoulder and holding it up. "I think it sends a positive message."

Her mother snorted. "Sure, the same message Muslims in Jerusalem received when they saw the large cross the crusaders charged behind."

Meghan's eyes narrowed in confusion. "I don't . . . "

"Never mind," her mother said, waving away the digression. "So what do we need to talk about?"

"Mom," Meghan said, pausing for dramatic effect. "I'm a pansexual."

Her mother stared at her.

Meghan reached across the table and grabbed her mother's hand. "Mom, did you hear me? I said I'm a pansexual."

"No, you're not," her mother said.

Meghan retreated back into her seat, shock evident across her face. "What do you mean? You can't say that!

I'm telling you I'm a pansexual. You can't just say 'No, you're not'!"

Her mother leaned back in her chair and folded her arms. The two stared at one another.

"So, you say you're a pansexual," her mother finally said.

"No, I'm not just saying that. I *am* that. I am a pansexual!"

Her mother rolled her eyes. "Prove it," she said.

Meghan stared at her mother.

"What? What do you mean, 'prove it'?" she said. "What do you expect me to do, make out with both a girl and a guy right in front of you?"

"That wouldn't prove you're a pansexual. That'd just prove you're a ... someone who is making bad moral decisions."

"I can't believe you told me to prove it like it's some kind of scientific experiment. I knew you wouldn't accept it. I knew you wouldn't accept me. You didn't act that way when Michael told you he was becoming a Catholic priest!"

"Thank you," her mother said. "Thank you for reminding me that both of my children have chosen to turn away from the religion I raised them in."

"That's not what I was saying," Meghan said. "I was just pointing out that you were supportive of Michael, even though he left your church. So why can't you be supportive of me?"

"Supportive?" her mother said. "Meghan, I cried every night for a week. I know he's an adult and can make his own decisions, but I always hoped ... anyway, and now you come to me and claim to be a pansexual ... "

"See, that's what I mean!" Meghan said. "You didn't

doubt Michael. You didn't ask him to prove anything. You accepted his decision! You accepted him."

Meghan's mother examined her for a moment before replying. "You really don't understand the difference, do you?"

Meghan shook her head. "All I want is for you to accept me."

"But I do accept you. You are my daughter. Of course I accept you. And I accept Michael, both of you. And I accept your right to choose your own path. You are adults now. I'll always hope of course ... but you are adults and I accept that. But I don't accept your truth claims, neither yours nor Michael's. And, frankly, you don't have the right to demand that I do."

"All I want is for you to accept me for who I am, a pansexual."

Her mother started to roll her eyes again but stopped halfway. "Okay, so what's a pansexual, Meghan? And don't give me someone else's Twit Tok definition. Tell me what you think a pansexual is."

"A pansexual is someone who is attracted to people regardless of their gender," Meghan said.

"Okay, and?"

"What do you mean, 'and'? That's it. I'm attracted to people regardless of their gender."

"Yes, but if that is all it means to be a pansexual, then I don't see what all the fuss is about, and I don't see how it causes an issue with the morals I raised you to follow either. So you're attracted to girls, too? So what? Ignore that attraction and go find a nice guy to marry."

"No, you don't understand," Meghan said. "I'm attracted to all genders! I'm a pansexual! It's who I am. You're asking me to reject who I am."

"Ah," her mother said, "and now we come to the point. According to you, a pansexual is more than just someone who is attracted to both genders. There are truth claims you're hiding in that word that you just expect me to accept."

"I don't understand what you mean."

"You aren't just saying that you're attracted to girls. You're saying that that attraction is who you *are*. That's a truth claim. Can you prove it?"

"Yes, because I'm a pansexual. That's the proof."

"No, that's circular reasoning. You're saying that your attraction to girls is part of who you are because you are a pansexual, and the proof of that is that you are a pansexual. The only thing that proves is I should have taught you better critical thinking skills."

"I can't believe we're arguing about this," Meghan said, throwing up her arms. "All I want is for you to accept what I am!"

"I accept that you believe you're a pansexual," her mother said.

"No, I *am* a pansexual. I want you to accept that I *am* a pansexual."

"I can't accept that," her mother said, "because what you're really asking me to do is to accept the truth claims you've embedded in that term. And I don't accept them. I think you're wrong, Meghan. I love you, but I think you're wrong."

Meghan shook her finger at her mother. "See!" She said. "You aren't showing me the respect you showed to Michael! You didn't tell him that you didn't believe he was a Catholic priest! You didn't tell him, 'I believe that you believe you're a Catholic priest!' "

"Why would I say that? He is a Catholic priest. That's

what he chose to become."

Meghan gaped at her Mom and shook her head. "You're going to just sit there calmly and admit that you're treating me differently than Michael. I can't believe this." She crossed her arms and glared.

Her mother looked down at the table and drummed her fingers for a moment. Then she looked back up at Meghan. "You really don't get it, do you?"

"I get that my mother doesn't accept me for who I am," Meghan said. "I get that you treat me like a second-class citizen."

"Meghan," her mother said, "what is a Catholic priest?"

"I'm not an idiot!" Meghan said. "You're just sitting there, rolling your eyes and asking me stupid questions."

Her mother held up her hands as a peace offering and gave a slight nod. "I admit that I've had a hard time taking some of what you said seriously, but I'm asking you a serious question here because I want to make a point. So tell me, what is a Catholic priest?"

"It's a man that's been ordained by the Catholic church," Meghan said. "I guess he takes confessions and gives the sacrament and stuff like that."

"And when Michael tells us that he's a Catholic priest, what does he expect us to accept?"

"That he's a Catholic priest! Just like I want you to accept that I'm a pansexual!"

"But put yourself in Michael's shoes," her mother said. "What does it mean to him to be a Catholic priest?"

"I don't know," Meghan said. "Why don't you ask him?"

"I don't need to ask him," her mother said, "because I already have. You know Michael. He does what he does because he believes it's right."

"So now you're saying that I don't do things I think are right?"

Her mother held up her hand. "We're talking about Michael here. Let me finish my point. Michael became a Catholic because he believes that religion is correct. He believes their truth claims. When he thinks of himself as a Catholic priest, he doesn't think of himself like we think of him—because we're not Catholics. But he is. He believes it. He believes he has been ordained with the priesthood of God, passed down through the Catholic church for centuries, all the way back to Peter. That's a truth claim of the Catholic church. That's a truth claim that Michael obviously believes."

"So?" Meghan said. "What does that have to do with you not accepting me?"

"Meghan," her mother said, "when Michael asks me to accept that he is a Catholic priest, does he expect me to accept all the truth claims about it that he has chosen to believe?"

"No."

"Exactly, and frankly he has never asked me to 'accept' that he *is* a Catholic priest. He told me he was converting to Catholicism and that he was becoming a priest. He wanted me to accept his choice, of course, but he didn't use those words."

"I don't understand the difference."

"The difference is the fence he allowed to be placed between us. Now sometimes the idea of a fence might seem negative, but think of the positive effect this has on our relationship. The fence separates our two yards, allowing us both to have our own. He, a Catholic, has his yard on his side of the fence. He can plant trees if he wants, or grass, or flowers, and he can do all that and still allow me, on my side of the fence, to tend my yard as I see fit. Don't you see? The fence between us is the respect we show to each other that we acknowledge that both of us have the right to believe what we choose to believe."

"But you don't want him to stay Catholic. You want him to return to your church."

"And I'm sure Michael would love for me to convert to Catholicism as well. That's natural. We love each other; of course we would want the other to believe the same way we do about God and the meaning of life. But we also respect each other, so we give each other the ability to believe differently."

"Then why don't you show me that same respect?"

"Meghan, you have completely misread the situation. I am willing to show you that same respect. I told you, I accept that you believe you're a pansexual. The problem here is that you aren't willing to show *me* that same respect."

"What are you talking about? I didn't say you had to change your religion. I just asked you to accept that I'm a pansexual."

"But the truth claims you've embedded into the word 'pansexual', the truth claims you are demanding I accept, are completely incompatible with my religion. I don't believe that same-sex attraction is part of who you *are*. You feel it sure, just like I feel lots of wrong desires, just like everyone does. But that isn't part of who we *are*."

"But it is who I am. I'm a pansexual! You're my mother and you're supposed to accept who I am!"

Her mother raised her hands in exasperation. "And there it is. You don't allow me the respect of a fence. You just march over into my yard and demand I let you rip up my grass so you can plant shrubs or trees or whatever you like in *my* yard. Well, you can't do that, Meghan. You don't have the right to do that. And frankly, I'm a little ashamed that I didn't teach you better so that you could understand that."

Meghan eyes stabbed at her mother. Silence filled the room.

"All I want," Meghan said in a low voice, "is to know if you will accept me for who I am. I am a pansexual, Mother. Don't you understand that I'm coming out to you? Don't you understand how important this moment is for me? I'm asking for your support. I'm asking for your acceptance."

Her mother sighed. "Meghan, I love you. You are my daughter, and I will always love you. But I don't believe our attractions define who we are. So I don't believe in pansexuality, not the way you believe in it. Just like I don't believe in Catholicism, not the way Michael believes in it. But I still love Michael, and I still love you, and I always will. But when you believe differently about the meaning of life than someone that you love, it's natural to always hope they will change their mind and come to agree with you. And I will always feel that way about you and about Michael. I'm your mother. I always will be."

"That's not good enough," Meghan said, rising from her chair. "If you really loved me, then you would accept me for what I really am. You're just a close-minded bigot. I'm ashamed you're my mother."

Meghan stormed out of the room, her rainbow ponytail trailing after her, the cape of a retreating crusader.

"I love you, Meghan!" her mother called after her. "I really do!"

The front door slammed

"Even when you're being a selfish, immature brat . . . "

The Freedom to Not Believe

Everyone must have the freedom to *not* believe.

If that statement seems anti-religious to you, then you aren't thinking widely enough. To believe is not always a positive thing. Some beliefs are wrong after all. And when a belief is wrong—when we *believe* a belief is wrong—we must have the freedom to *not* believe it.

Now, if something is provable, then that is a different matter. But everything I will discuss here, all of the beliefs, all of the truth claims, all of them are unprovable. Which means that all of them are based entirely on faith.

In my last satire, "The Coming Out", Meghan's mother asks her the question: "What is a Catholic priest?" The question is a simple one, but if you ponder the answer, and if you consider it from both a Catholic and a non-Catholic perspective, I think you will be able to better perceive the societal regression the LGBT movement represents. And I'm not talking about morality here. Yes, the moral problems caused by that movement are concerning, but they are not as devastating as the attack on freedom the LGBT movement represents, an attack on our freedom to *not* believe.

"Cuius regio, eius religio" or in other words "whose realm, his religion". Go back in time a few hundred years in Europe and you will understand the bondage expressed by that phrase. How would you like to have to believe in whatever religion your king belonged to? Are you a Protestant but your king is a Catholic? Too bad, you don't have the right to *not* believe. Are you a Catholic but your king is a Protestant? Too bad, you don't have the right to *not* believe. And then bloody war after bloody war, murder, atrocities of all kinds. And finally, western civilization started to learn its lesson. Enlightenment, modernity, the concept of *individual* religious freedom, the freedom to believe, the freedom to *not* believe.

And it is that freedom, the freedom to *not* believe, that the LGBT movement is trying to steal from us. It is a regression to the bad old days of religious belief imposed by force. "Cuius regio, eius religio."

"But that isn't the same at all! The LGBT movement is secular! It isn't a religious movement!"

Ah, quite a clever tactic that is ...

But let's return to my question, "What is a Catholic priest?" Because the true answer is: It depends.

Depends? Depends on what?

It depends on who is answering the question. A Catholic priest means one thing to a non-Catholic, and quite another to a Catholic. To a Catholic, a Catholic priest isn't simply a man who holds a position in their church. No, this is a man who has been ordained into the ministerial priesthood of God. This is a man with the authority to perform sacred rites, rites which have efficacy on the destination of the human soul. This is a man who holds an authority passed down through the centuries from Peter, and who did Peter receive it from?

From Christ, from God Himself, meaning that yes there is a God, a Divine Creator, and a purpose to existence, and punishment, and reward, and truth.

Consider all those truth claims, and ask yourself this question: Do I have to believe that?

No, you don't. You don't have to believe any of it. You have the freedom to *not* believe.

And would any Catholic disagree? I would hope not. This isn't the 16th century anymore, or the 17th. Western civilization has learned bitter lessons about the importance of *individual* religious freedom.

And to be clear, this freedom that everyone has to *not* believe extends to all religions, including my own. I am a member of the Church of Jesus Christ of Latter-day Saints. Do you have to believe the truth claims I believe in? Do you have to believe in the Book of Mormon? Do you have to believe in modern-day prophets? Do you have to believe that I, like many Latter-day Saint men, have been ordained to the priesthood? No, you don't. You have the freedom to *not* believe.

"But you are talking about religions! The LGBT movement isn't a religious movement!"

Ah, yes, quite clever. Well then, please tell me: What is a pansexual? What is a gay man? What is a transgender? Because that is the key, isn't it? What truth claims are you embedding into those terms? And are those truth claims provable or unprovable? And do we have the freedom to *not* believe?

Tell me, if a state decides to forbid transgender boys who believe they are girls from competing in girls sports, does that discriminate against transgenders?

"Yes!"

But how can that be? Is it discrimination to say that

boys can't play in girls sports?

"No, of course not."

Then I'm confused because this is a boy, which means that like all other boys, he shouldn't be allowed to play in girls sports.

"No, this is a transgender! This is a girl!"

Ah, and so we come to the truth claim. And can you prove this boy is a girl? No, you can't. Your declaration that this boy is a girl is not based on anything empirical. It isn't falsifiable. It is simply a statement of self-identity.

And do we have the right to not believe in that self-identity? Do we have the freedom to *not* believe in that unprovable belief?

No, according to the LGBT movement, we don't have that freedom. According to the LGBT movement, we don't have the freedom to *not* believe.

Anytime there is a claim of anti-LGBT discrimination, strip away the unprovable truth claims embedded into the various sexual and gender identifies and ask yourself if that claim of discrimination makes any sense anymore. Chances are, it won't.

Let's consider an analogy:

If a Catholic priest walked into a Latter-day Saint church and demanded to be able to perform the baptisms there and was told no, is that discrimination? No, not unless you require the world to believe the unprovable truth claim that he actually has priesthood authority to perform baptisms.

Now let's apply that to the LGBT movement:

If a transgender boy demands to play on the girls team and is told no, is that discrimination? No, not unless you require the world to believe the unprovable truth claim that he actually is a girl.

If a pansexual demands that her conservative private university must drop its rules against same-sex sexuality, and they say no, is that discrimination? No, not unless you require the world to believe the unprovable truth claim that her same-sex attraction actually is a core part of who she is instead of simply a wrong desire she can choose to reject.

With Catholic priests (and all other religious roles), we have learned to separate the truth claims from the label. We need to learn to do the same with all of the LGBT labels as well. Of course, that would mean the end of the LGBT movement as we know it because that's the core of what the LGBT movement actually is: crusaders charging against the "infidels", conversions attained by force, the destruction of any resistance. The LGBT movement would be greatly diminished if everyone exercised their freedom to *not* believe. That is why it is working so hard to take that freedom away.

Have you ever considered how beautiful the concept of religion is? No, I'm not trying to rehash the tired argument "Is organized religion good or bad?" What I'm talking about is the *concept* of religion, the idea that I can take all of my unprovable truth claims and I can package them together into a neat little bundle, and you can package your unprovable truth claims into your own neat little bundle, and despite our differences, the two of us can get along just fine. Sure, we believe different things about life, but those are all packaged into our neat little bundles, and you have your bundle, and I have mine, and maybe you're a Catholic, and maybe I'm a Latter-day Saint, and maybe someone else is a Muslim, and maybe someone else is a Jew, and yet we can all get along civilly, respecting each other's right to believe as we see fit, and respecting each other's right to *not* believe as well.

Or maybe you don't think the concept of religion is beautiful. Maybe you hate the idea that people are allowed to believe differently than you. Because your beliefs are right, aren't they, and everyone else's beliefs are wrong, aren't they? Not just wrong but horrible, hateful! And why would we want to give people the right to believe wrong, hateful beliefs? Think of how much discrimination that can cause. Think of how much injustice, of how much bigotry!

And if you have the power, you can force your will on us all. And so we return to "Cuius regio, eius religio" don't we? And so we regress and unlearn all the lessons we learned through so much blood and horror, hatred and death. Because those of you who want to strip other's freedom of belief away are not really thinking this through, are you? "Whose realm, his religion" — fine words, when *you* are the one in charge. But why do you assume you will always be in charge? And when you're not, what then? Will you finally understand how important it is to be free to *not* believe?

Imagine if the Catholic religion disappeared tomorrow, not the Catholic *beliefs*, the Catholic *religion.* In other words, the beliefs remain, but the concept of religion is gone, so what was once understood to be a religious belief is now treated like secular *fact.* So let's return to the question, "What is a Catholic priest?" Remember all those unprovable truth claims listed above? Before they were all safely bundled together into that wonderful package of religion, a religion you can choose to accept, a religion you can choose to reject. But when that concept of religion is gone yet the unprovable truth claims remain ... what then?

Ah, but we already know, don't we? Because we are living through it today. Tell me: What is a pansexual? What is a gay man? What is a transgender?

Answer my question, and then tell me this: Do I have the freedom to *not* believe?

Gender Identity and the Invisible Pasta God

Kale was a twenty-year-old virgin and that was just freaking unacceptable. Oh, it's not that he hadn't tried. You have no idea how hard he'd tried, the dozens of first dates in high school: dinners, movies, dances. And how many second dates had that translated into? Less than you could count on one hand. And how many third dates? A big fat zero. Kale had been friend-zoned more times than he could count, been "like a brother" to half the girls in his graduating class, and altogether been the most non-nice guy to have ever been afflicted with the "nice guy" curse.

Now Kale was in his second "gap year" between high school and college, adrift, no aspirations in his life, nothing going for him except a bi-weekly paycheck from Infinite Word Worlds, the only remaining bookstore in his town, where he worked the day shift. He spent the night shift alone, assuaging his loneliness through pixels on his computer monitor. Sunrise followed by sunset. Rinse and repeat.

But no more. Last night, Kale had discovered inspiration. Last night, Kale had had a revelation. Not a boring, stuffy revelation you might hear about from your ninety-seven-year-old Sunday School teacher. Not a vision, not a voice, not a bright light, a burning bush, or a talking donkey. No, Kale's revelation had come from that most accurate of sources: the Internet. There he had been, just like every other night, jumping from site to site, as was his habit, demonstrating his manhood to himself through the sheer variety of bodies he might objectify, when he had discovered that which would turn his life around, give him purpose, and translate the digital ones and zeros he fixated on into real flesh and blood objects he could use and leisurely discard. Praise be, Kale had discovered a pickup artist message forum.

These were giants among men, Michelangelos who nightly crafted masterpieces of personal pleasure out of willing canvases of makeup, hairspray, and low self-esteem. The notches on these men's bedposts were legendary: dozens ... hundreds. It was awe inspiring. Did a single night go by when these men among men were not bagging a new conquest? Was there a woman alive who was immune to their charisma and their carefully choreographed playbook that was guaranteed to transform ice queens into raging volcanoes? Kale didn't think so, and the thought made his palms sweat.

Could he really be like them? Could he exude testosterone like some bathroom dispenser of male musk? Could he follow in the footsteps of such heroes of the pickup artist message forum like AlphaAlphaInfinity, LadySlayerX304, or NeggingMasterW? They claimed he could! To think that a beta male like him could reach such heights of alphaness, it was wonderful. And the steps were all right there on the Internet! All explained through message post after message post, or available as downloadable lectures for the low cost of three of his paychecks.

The pickup artists had byzantine levels of seduction. If a woman was here, then you should do this to raise her to the next level. If that didn't work, then try this. It was all very complicated, and in truth it was a little too much for Kale to understand, especially after only one night of study. But he did remember a few key points.

The first was negging. The idea was simple: you insult a woman until her self-esteem is so battered and broken that she'll be willing to have sex with you. Some pickup artists like NeggingMasterW seemed to have raised it to an art form. He had once negged the valedictorian of an Ivy League college on graduation night, only hours after her valedictory speech. The evening had started with her riding high on confidence, being honored in front of hundreds of people, and had ended with NeggingMasterW riding her, the valedictorian reduced to just one more notch on his bedpost. No woman could resist a master of negging.

The second was the touching technique. It was named something that started with a "k". Kino? Kilo? Kale couldn't remember. He just thought of it as the touching technique. The idea was to make progressively more and more physical contact with the woman you desire, getting her used to your presence and moving her along the path to hooking up with you, all the while trying your hardest to not give her the impression that you're a creep. LadySlayerX304 had written hundreds of words on the topic. Kale had only skimmed the guidelines, but he thought he had the gist of it.

Before the night was over, he had already decided on his first target: his co-worker Jezzie. She was a recent hire, and he hadn't worked up the nerve to actually speak to her yet, but she was young and the only cute girl who worked at the bookstore, and given Kale's recent lack of socialization outside of work, she was his best bet.

Jezzie shaved her head, which was weird and honestly lowered her a few points on the bangable scale, but she was still sufficiently hot to be the first notch on his bedpost; and at the same time, thanks to her shaved head, she wasn't extremely hot, so Kale wouldn't be too intimidated to try out his pickup artist techniques for the first time.

And so Kale found himself the next day near the end of his shift, peeking out from behind a bookshelf at Jezzie, who was sitting on the floor next to a pile of books in the religious books section. Kale tried to work up the courage to approach her. AlphaAlphaInfinity said you should swallow your fear and let your body convert it into testosterone, which sounded easy when looking at pictures of women on the computer screen, but turned out to be not quite so easy when faced with a real flesh and blood woman in real life.

Kale struggled to think of an opener, something, anything, to break the ice and put her on the path toward becoming a notch on his bedpost, but his mind was blank. What would LadySlayerX304 say? How about NeggingMasterW? Kale couldn't think of anything. And as he stood there, hiding behind a bookshelf in the self-help section, the excitement he had felt the night before slowly morphed into despair. Who was he kidding? Kale was pathetic and he knew it. He wasn't just a beta. He was an omega. The lowest of the low. He would die a virgin and his obituary would only have three words: "What a loser."

"Hey, can you help me with this?"

Kale froze and for a moment he worried he might have wet himself. Jezzie was staring up at him. "Can you help me with this?" she repeated.

"Uh, sure," Kale said, forcing himself to move forward.

Swallow your fear and turn it into testosterone. Swallow your fear and turn it into testosterone. Kale could do this. He was sure he could. And sure enough he made it the six feet to where Jezzie sat. Bending over, he bravely picked up a translation of the Bible and stuffed it on the shelf with the rest of the Bibles. Here he was, standing next to the woman who would be in his bed by the end of the night. Kale's despair was forgotten, replaced by excitement over what might be to come. But how to open? NeggingMasterW always opened with a neg. That sounded like a good idea, so Kale said the first insult that came to mind.

"You look too smart to be here in the religious books section."

It was a crappy neg. Kale recognized that as soon as he had said it. Sure, there was the little insinuation that, because she was in the religious books section, she must be stupid, but the related compliment was too large, making the neg lopsided.

Jezzie just shrugged. "The manager told me to shelve these books."

"Oh," Kale said, disappointed in himself that he had failed his first neg. Surely there should be something he could say to insult her? Something about her looks maybe? Girls cared so much about their looks it was a great way to bash their self-esteem. Maybe something with her clothes? The bookstore had a casual clothing policy and, like Kale, Jezzie was wearing a t-shirt and jeans, but Kale couldn't see anything wrong with what she had on, nothing he could neg her about.

"Although, if you ask me," Jezzie said. "We should be filing all these religious books in the fiction section, don't you think?

"Uh, yeah," Kale said, noncommittally. He still couldn't think of a neg. He was standing so close to her, he could smell her faint perfume. It was all so overwhelming. How could a man insult a woman who was so attractive? But he had to. There was a neg he could say. There had to be. Maybe something about being too stupid to understand the book classification system? No, no, that had no style. How did pickup artist masters like AlphaAlphaInfinity do it? They made it seem so easy. This felt like actual work.

"I was watching a documentary on religion last night," Jezzie said. "Hilarious. I haven't laughed so loud in my life."

I'll bet you have a stupid laugh. Kale tested the neg out in his head. No, no, no! This was hopeless. He couldn't think of a neg here in the heat of battle. He needed time to think. He needed time to prepare. But all was not lost. There was still the touching technique. The pickup artists in the message forum had discussed it at length. To start he had to touch her in a nonthreatening way. He should make it seem almost accidental, like it meant nothing to him. And then the next touch would be more significant, and then more, and then more, and then she'd be in his bed—but he was getting ahead of himself.

Where to touch her first? He considered putting a hand on her shoulder. That seemed normal enough. But with her sitting on the ground and him standing up, Kale worried he might fall over. He considered other options but none presented themselves. He would have to go for it. And so, swallowing his fear, he moved his hand toward her shoulder. But right before he could touch it she leaned forward to place a book on the shelf, leaving Kale's hand sitting alone in the air. Not wanting to look like an idiot, he patted her shaved head.

"Did you just pat me on the head like a dog?" Jezzie asked.

Kale stepped back and cleared his throat, clasping his hands behind his back. "Yeah, religions are all pretty hilarious, aren't they?" he said, trying to pretend the last few seconds hadn't happened.

Jezzie looked at him for a moment and then smiled. "You're a funny guy. What's your name again?"

"Kale" he said. And you're funny looking, he thought, but he didn't say the neg out loud. He felt like such an idiot.

"Well, my name's Jezzie"

Why did her name matter? It's not like he'd be bagging her tonight anyway. Kale had failed the pickup artist brotherhood. He was a failure, a loser, an omega male forever. His obituary was pre-written: "What a loser." It would probably be carved on his tombstone too, a big neon sign pointing down to where the loser was bur—

"Hey, do you have plans tonight?" Jezzie asked him.

A dizzying procession of emotions overcame Kale. First, he worried again that he might have wet himself, but then it was as if a light shone down from above and church choirs broke into singing all around. AlphaAlphaInfinity, LadySlayerX304, NeggingMasterW, you are all geniuses! The Pulitzer Prize, the Noble Prize, the Powerball lottery—all of them, you deserve! He hadn't even done the negging or the touching technique right and yet here she was, practically begging him to bed her.

"No," Kale answered, but then he reconsidered. Think like an alpha, think like an alpha, he reminded himself. "I mean, yeah, but it's no biggie. Why," he asked casually, "what did you have in mind?"

"There's a Pastafarian meetup scheduled at the civic center," she said. "It's supposed to be a lot of fun. Mocking the religious, awesome, right? But I've never been, and I would feel weird showing up all by myself. Want to come with me?"

"Sure," Kale said, "a Pastafarian meetup sounds fine. And then we could ... " But he wasn't brave enough to finish the sentence, so he left it hanging, hoping she would fill it in. She didn't.

"You know about Pastafarians, right?" Jezzie asked.

"Of course," Kale said, assuming it was some sort of carbohydrate-heavy dinner party.

"Great! It'll be fun. And hilarious! I'm off at six and it starts at seven. I'll meet you there. Civic center, like I said."

It wasn't exactly a date, but Kale would take would he could get. It was a solid beginning, and he was super optimistic about the ending. He didn't know what this Pastafarian thing was, and frankly he didn't care, but it sounded like it should include dinner, so he wouldn't have to worry about eating beforehand. He'd spend the hours from now until then coming up with some really confidence-destroying negs. He'd be more assertive and alpha-like in his touching technique, and before you know it, he'd have left his virginity behind and gotten the first notch on his bedpost.

Kale arrived half an hour early at the civic center, an ugly brown building surrounded by lackluster landscaping. He peeked into room 5b, where the announcement board in the hallway said the Pastafarian meetup was scheduled to occur, but no one was there yet. There was a bench outside the room, and Kale considered waiting there, but he decided that would make him look too desperate. He needed Jezzie to be desperate, not him. That was the whole point of being a pickup artist: making the girls desperate enough to give you exactly what you want. He had already figured out the perfect neg, one that would lower her self-esteem to the gutter and make her beg him to lift it back up.

Wanting to be out of sight when Jezzie arrived, Kale hid in a janitors closet down the hall. It was dark and smelled like something small and disease-ridden had crawled into a corner and died, but beggars couldn't be choosers, so Kale ignored the smell as he peeked through the crack between the door and doorframe and watched everyone walk past. His stomach began to growl. These Pastafarians had better have some good food, Kale thought, because he had skipped dinner for this.

After twenty-five minutes of waiting, Kale began to wonder if Jezzie had played a trick on him. It figured, he thought. Why did girls always treat nice guys like him so bad? But then he reminded himself he wasn't just some beta-male nice guy anymore. He was a pickup artist now. And he had thought of the perfect neg to use on her. If only she would actually show up . . .

His heart leapt when he saw Jezzie finally walk past the janitors closet. She had actually came! Jezzie was carrying something loud and bulky in a shopping bag that clanged against her leg with each step. Kale counted to ten after she passed and then scurried out of the closet and called her name right before she went into the meeting room.

"Oh, where'd you come from?" Jezzie asked. "I didn't see you in the hall."

"I just got here," Kale lied leisurely.

He opened the door for her to enter the room, then he

wondered if pickup artists were supposed to do such things for their conquests. He would have to seek the wisdom of AlphaAlphaInfinity and the other pickup artist masters from the Internet message forum later. Hopefully by then he'd have an exploit of his own to brag to them about.

The room was small, setup with two rows of faded orange plastic chairs arranged in a semicircle. The tile on the floor was old and scarred. The walls were faded white, with posters of various community events or public announcements scattered here and there. All in all, the place reeked of bureaucracy and boredom.

There were a handful of people in the room now. Everyone was sitting apart from each other, no one talking. Kale understood now why Jezzie didn't want to come here alone. They didn't seem like the friendliest bunch. He scanned the room, paying attention first to the men. The pickup artist message forum had made it clear how important it was to be the alpha male in the room. All of these men were his competition one way or another. He would have to assert his alphaness over all of them ... somehow.

Of course he spent time checking out all the women as well. None were particularly hot, certainly nowhere close to Jezzie on the bangable scale, even with her shaved head. Sure, he would have gone for some of them on a normal day, but today was not a normal day. Today he was guided by the wisdom of greats like AlphaAlphaInfinity and LadySlayerX304. Today he had no reason to be desperate or to settle for anyone that wasn't sufficiently hot, and Jezzie certainly was sufficiently hot.

Kale and Jezzie sat down at one end of the back row, their seats next to each other. Kale subtly scooted his chair slightly closer, causing their shoulders to touch. Jezzie didn't flinch at this, so Kale figured it kind of counted as the first level of the touching technique. He was getting the hang of this.

Kale had come dressed for the kill. He had worn his best dark polo shirt and had matched it with his only pair of clean khaki pants. Jezzie, on the other hand, hadn't changed since work. She still wore the t-shirt and jeans she had been wearing earlier. He could smell her perfume once again. It was intoxicating. There was a little bit of sweat stink mixed in there too—she obviously hadn't taken the time to freshen up after a full day of work—but Kale chose to ignore that. Things were going great. Here he was, sitting next to her, shoulders touching. Now was the time for the awesome neg he had planned all afternoon. It was about her looks, the best kind of neg for a woman, and Kale was positive it would have the desired effect.

Kale leaned back in his chair with forced casualness and looked over at Jezzie. Injecting a cocky swagger into his voice he had never used before, he said, "You must be really confident to choose such an unattractive hairstyle."

Kale smiled inwardly and congratulated himself on his perfect delivery. Negging wasn't so hard. He might actually finally be getting the hang of this! NeggingMasterW would be proud.

Jezzie frowned and was quiet for a moment. Kale imagined her turning to him, desperation in her beautiful brown eyes. "Oh, Kale," he imagined her saying. "I need a strong man like you to make me feel better about myself." Kale would then put his arm around her shoulder and say, "How about we stop delaying the inevitable and just head back to my place and get it on?" To which Jezzie would reply "Oh, yes! Oh, yes! I thought you'd never ask!"

But that wasn't quite how the conversation went. Instead of following Kale's fantasy, Jezzie said, "My little sister has cancer and I shaved my head to support her."

Alarms blared inside Kale's head. DANGER! DANGER! NEW SUBJECT! NEW SUBJECT! In his mind he formed a little checklist of pickup artists do's and don'ts and in the first line he wrote, highlighted, bolded, and underlined: "Don't ever neg a woman about her shaved head. She probably has a family member with cancer." He worried he might have ruined everything. Desperately, he tried to change the subject. "That sucks, so, uh, what do you have in your shopping bag?"

Jezzie's frown didn't go away, and frankly she looked a little pissed, but she lifted up her shopping bag and opened it, showing what was inside: two metal colanders, shiny and new from the store. Kale figured they would be used to strain the pasta for the Pastafarian dinner party, although now that he came to think of it, there were no tables or stoves or anything of that nature in the room. How were they supposed to eat? His stomach gave a soft rumble.

And then Kale had a moment of inspiration. All this time he had been fixated on just two of the techniques in the pickup artist's arsenal, but there was far more to it than that. He remembered a third technique AlphaAlphaInfinity had given advice about: peacocking. The idea was simple: just like a male peacock spread its tail feathers to stand out from the crowd and assert its alphaness, so too could a pickup artist dress or act in a way to make him standout, thereby heightening his attractiveness and transforming women into putty in his hands.

Kale swallowed his fear before he had time to second guess himself. Quickly he leaned over and grabbed one of the colanders from Jezzie's shopping bag, then with the confidence of AlphaAlphaInfinity, LadySlayerX304, and

NeggingMasterW all rolled together into one unstoppable alpha male, Kale put the colander on his head. Turning to Jezzie, he gave her his best flirty smile. "So, how do I look?"

And it worked! Jezzie's frown and anger melted away. She actually laughed! Kale couldn't believe how great things were going. Pickup artists truly were geniuses. Was there anything they couldn't accomplish?

Then Jezzie reached into the bag and pulled out the other colander. She placed it on her own head, just like Kale had done, and turned and smiled at him.

This was unexpected and Kale was confused. Was she trying to peacock as well? Did girls do that sort of thing?

He heard a nervous giggle from one of the others in the room, and one by one everyone else reached into bags or backpacks, pulled out colanders, and placed them on their heads.

What in the world had he gotten himself into? Kale wondered. Now they were all wearing colanders on their heads. How was he supposed to peacock in a room full of people that were peacocking just as well?

"So you do know about Pastafarians," Jezzie said.

"Uh, yeah, of course," Kale said, wondering if he should keep the silly thing on his head now that everyone else in the room was wearing the same thing. A young man on the opposite side of the room had put a fake plastic eye patch over one eye. A woman in the first row quietly put some sort of long beaded belt around her waist.

"Ridiculous," Jezzie giggled. "Don't you get it?" she said, pointing at the colander on her head. "It's just like the clothing real religions wear. Ridiculous! If they get to wear their silly stuff, then we get to wear silly stuff too. That's why we wear colanders on our heads. It's a sign of respect for the Flying Spaghetti Monster."

"The Flying Spaghetti Monster?" Kale said, and his stomach grumbled at the mention of food.

"Of course, I thought you said you knew about Pastafarians?"

"Yeah, a little," Kale said, beginning to realize that there might be no dinner party after all. His stomach whined in protest.

"It was about a decade ago," Jezzie said. "Some Midwest hick state, probably Kansas—it sounds like something Kansas would do, doesn't it?"

Kale shrugged his shoulders, having no idea what she was talking about. He had to get things moving in the right direction again. But how? Did he dare try another neg? He had messed up his last one, and that was after hours of preparation! And peacocking didn't appear to work in a room full of people who wore colanders on their heads for fun. Time to try the touching technique again, Kale decided.

Jezzie went on: "Anyway, in Kansas about a decade ago, they decided they should teach Intelligent Design in their classrooms alongside evolution. Can you imagine that? Intelligent Design being taught in a public school right there along with evolution. Ridiculous!"

Kale stared at her blankly.

"You know what Intelligent Design is, right?" Jezzie asked.

Kale shrugged again. His mind was preoccupied on his next line of attack. He couldn't be too forward. That might creep her out. He had to be sneaky about it. Yet at the same time, he had to somehow make her want more. Her elbow seemed like a safe bet. Jezzie's looked tan and inviting.

"Intelligent Design is just Creationism, dressed up to pretend to be a scientific theory. But it's not scientific at all. It's pure religion," Jezzie said. "Of course it's religion. Science can be proven. Science is based on empirical evidence. You know, stuff you can see, feel, touch; stuff you can measure. That's science. And Intelligent Design isn't science. 'It's all too complicated for evolution to be true. Evolution couldn't have created life in this complicated manner.' That's what Intelligent Design says. 'So there must have been a creator,' they say. And we're supposed to just believe them. No proof! No evidence! Just believe them because they say it's true, like their words should overrule physical reality!"

"Uh-huh," Kale said. Jezzie was sitting to his right, their shoulders still brushing together. He decided that touching her left elbow would be the best next step. Leaning over her body to touch her right elbow would just be too weird, and the colander might fall off his head. What if he lightly brushed her left elbow with the fingertips of his right hand? Would that work? She might think it was just accidental. Would that be good? Would that be bad? Or should he reach across and grab her left elbow lightly with his left hand, making it obvious he was touching her? That seemed more alpha-like, but was it too soon? He wished he could consult with AlphaAlphaInfinity, LadySlayerX304, or NeggingMasterW. He needed their advice.

"Do you know how you can tell someone is preaching religion to you?" Jezzie asked him.

Kale muttered a non-committal reply. He would lightly grab her left elbow with his left hand. Bold. Brave. Alpha-like. This was going to be great. Swallow your fear and let your body convert it into testosterone. That's what AlphaAlphaInfinity would say. And AlphaAlphaInfinity was a master at this. Holding his breath, Kale started to lift his left hand.

But then Jezzie's body tensed and she raised her left elbow to her nose, letting out a huge sneeze. "Excuse me!" she said. She lowered her elbow back down beside Kale. "You know someone is preaching religion to you when they tell you to believe something that contradicts your own eyes. That's religion for you!" she said.

Kale stared at Jezzie's left elbow, imagining the millions of molecules of snot and germs she had just contaminated it with. He dropped his left hand back down. Foiled again. It's like the universe hated him.

Jezzie just kept on talking. "So when Kansas wanted to teach Intelligent Design in public schools, that was obviously wrong. Religion doesn't belong in public schools. Public schools are supposed to be secular. But they kept arguing that it was reasonable, blah, blah, blah, masquerading their religious beliefs like they were scientific."

Kale imagined the hundreds of alphas who posted on the pickup artist message forum. They were all probably out prowling the city right now, scoring again and again with nines and tens on the bangable scale when he couldn't even score with a girl who shaved her head. What was he supposed to do now? Grab her other elbow? Go for the knee?

"Anyway," Jezzie continued, "there was this guy, I forget his name. Genius. Hilarious. He's the one that came up with the Flying Spaghetti Monster. He wrote an open letter to the Kansas school board, explaining it was just as reasonable to believe that the earth was created by an invisible Flying Spaghetti Monster as it was to believe it was created by Intelligent Design. So if they were going to teach Intelligent Design in the classroom, they should teach about the Flying Spaghetti Monster as well. After all, they both had the same amount of proof. Brilliant!"

Kale's stomach jumped at the mention of spaghetti. He really regretted not grabbing a before-meetup snack.

"And that's the whole point of Pastafarianism," Jezzie said. "It's a way to highlight the difference between science and religion and to point out the ridiculousness of religion. If you can't prove it, then it's not science. If it goes against what you can see or measure, then it's not science. I mean seriously, we have all these fossils lying around, which are carbon-dated back millions of years, and what do Creationists say about them? They say God put them there just to confuse us or something like that, so that's what Pastafarians say too! The Flying Spaghetti Monster placed the fossils in the ground to confuse us. He did it to test our faith. See how it works? And anytime a scientist makes a measurement—to perform carbon dating or something like that—the Flying Spaghetti Monster reaches down from the heavens and alters it. Imagine a stringy spaghetti noodle reaching down and changing scientists' measurements. Except he's invisible, so you can't see it, and the Pastafarians call it a noodly appendage instead of just a noodle because that makes it sound more formal and religious-like. So he reaches down with his noodly appendage and changes scientific measurements to make the Earth appear older than it really is, and he does it to test our faith."

Jezzie adjusted the colander on her head. "And that's the point of Pastafarianism: mocking the religious and stopping people from passing off religious beliefs as scientific ones, because if there is just as much objective evidence for the Flying Spaghetti Monster as there is for your own beliefs, then it's obvious your beliefs are religious, not scientific. So they wear colanders on their heads and dress like pirates. Oh, I didn't explain that part, did I? They dress like pirates because pirates are the Flying Spaghetti Monster's chosen people. I forget why, but I'm sure there's a funny reason. So dressing like a pirate is another way to show respect to him."

That explained the cheesy plastic eye patch the guy on the other side of the room was wearing. Perhaps that explained the beaded belt the woman on the front row had put on as well. Kale wasn't sure since he didn't know much about pirate garb. But really, none of that nonsense mattered. The only important thing was getting Jezzie in bed with him and as for how to achieve that, Kale was at a loss. He didn't dare touch her knee or reach across her body and grab her other elbow. That just seemed too advanced. And her left elbow was contaminated with germs and nastiness. Could he somehow change seats with her? Then he could go for her right elbow more subtly.

Jezzie looked around the room. Everyone was quietly waiting. "I wonder when it will start?" she said to Kale. Then she leaned close and whispered in Kale's ear, causing him to tense nervously. "Do you think the other women here are lady pirates, or do you think they are wenches?"

Kale had no idea how to respond. Was she coming on to him? Were the pickup artist techniques actually working? But how? Nothing had gone right! His perfect neg had backfired, his peacocking hadn't accomplished anything, and touching her elbow now would probably put him in the ER. But here she was whispering in his ear about wenches. Was she trying to tell him something?

Jezzie kept whispering in his ear. "Pastafarianism was made up by a guy—Pastafarian heaven has a beer volcano and a stripper factory, that explains that, right? And there's a lot of talk about pirates getting wenches, which is great for guys, but kind of awkward for girls. So I wondered, do the women Pastafarians think of themselves as lady pirates, or do they think of themselves just as wenches for the Pastafarian guys?"

Kale knew exactly how he wanted Jezzie to think of herself, but how could he get her there? Perhaps another neg? She seemed too confident right now to be willing to give it up to him. Kale wasn't a fool. He knew he was just pretending to be an alpha. The truth was he was an omega at heart. No smart, self-confident woman would ever go for him, not until he had knocked her self-esteem down a few levels. But he had to do it with style, with finesse. He couldn't just make Jezzie mad like last time. He thought of his heroes, those incredible alpha men who graced the pickup artist message forum with their wisdom, masters of the female psyche like AlphaAlphaInfinity, LadySlayerX304, and NeggingMasterW. What would they do? Kale's stomach rumbled.

The door slammed opened and Kale's miserably empty stomach jumped in surprise. Everyone in the room turned around. There in the open doorway stood an old pirate. The man had sun-wrinkled caucasian skin and gray hair spilling out of his blue tricorn hat. He wore a faded eye patch over his left eye, real leather not cheap plastic, and he had large gold hoop earrings which hung from each ear, reaching down half the length of his gray, scraggly beard. His rough white shirt with ruffled sleeves was tucked into baggy black trousers that had vertical stripes, and when he started walking toward the front of the room, Kale's mouth dropped open. The old pirate had a peg leg. He had a real bleeping peg leg! There is peacocking and then there is peacocking ... Wow! AlphaAlphaInfinity had nothing on this guy.

But any comparison to the heroic pickup artists from the message forum faded away when Kale saw the woman who followed closely behind the pirate. She appeared to be pushing ninety years old, with white hair and wrinkly caucasian skin sagging out of her cheap "Sexy Pirate" costume. The peg-legged pirate looked like he'd just stepped off a pirate ship. This woman looked like she'd just walked out of a Halloween store. She was a walking argument to putting a maximum age limit on such skimpy costumes, and she followed after the peg-legged pirate like a love-struck puppy, making it clear she saw herself not as a lady pirate but as this old pirate's wench.

The peg-legged pirate strode quickly to the front of the room (as quick as a man with a real bleeping peg leg can stride) and help up a piece of paper for the whole room to see. His pirate wench stood to his side, slightly behind him, and declared loudly. "See his certificate!"

"Aye, me mateys," the old pirate said. "See me certificate, printed fresh from the Internet this afternoon, declaring me, yer humble pirate, an official Pastafarian minister."

"An official Pastafarian Minister!" the pirate wench echoed.

"Aye, and thereby worthy to speak to ye, me mateys, about His Noodliness," the minister said.

"His Noodliness!" the pirate wench echoed.

"Arr. The Noodly Creator has touched me with His Noodly Appendage. Perhaps He has touched ye as well. I see ye all are wearing yer colanders, showing proper respect to the Flying Spaghetti Monster as ye should."

All the Pastafarians in the audience nodded and smiled at each other.

"This is so awesome!" Jezzie whispered to Kale.

The minister folded his certificate and placed it in a pocket. Then he raised his arms out wide and spoke with enthusiasm. "Do ye want to be taught about the Flying Spaghetti Monster?"

No one was brave enough to answer.

The pirate scowled. Clearly he was expecting more enthusiasm. A small fire burned in his unpatched eye, revealing that this was a pirate with a nasty streak. The pirate wench glared at the small group. "Answer him! Answer him!" she said shrilly.

"Uh, yes," said the young man with the fake eye patch.

"What was that?" the minister asked.

"Um, I mean, aye?" the young man said. Other members of the group, including Kale, offered their mumbled agreement.

The minister relaxed and the pirate wench returned her fawning attention back on him. He began to walk back and forth in front of the room, his peg leg making a distinct clunk with each step. "And what should be said about His Noodliness? Do ye know what He looks like?" The minister clunked a few steps. "Ha! That be a trick question for He be invisible!"

"Invisible!" the pirate wench echoed.

"Aye, invisible," the minister said, "and able to pass through walls like they be air. Yet we do know what He looks like for He hath revealed it onto us. The Flying Spaghetti Monster, His Great Noodliness, doth be a tangled clump of spaghetti, with two glorious eyestalks atop Himself, and two large meatballs. Can ye imagine … can ye imagine the glory of His being? Can ye imagine the power of His Noodly Appendages?"

The minister clunked back and forth in front of the

room for a moment while the Pastafarians basked in the wonder of the Flying Spaghetti Monster. Kale, for his part, wished the Pastafarian minister would stop mentioning spaghetti so much. It made him hungry.

"And this Glorious Being," the minister went on, "this Carbohydrate-Rich Celestial Entity, does He just sit yonder in the heavens and relax and watch the comets go by? No!"

"No!" the pirate wench echoed.

"For He created the universe," the minister said, "the Earth, everything in it. All of this only a few thousand years ago. Can ye imagine? And then He rearranged things, making everything appear to be older than it truly be. The fossils in the ground—ye know of the fossils in the ground, do ye not?"

"Aye!" many Pastafarians replied, laughing.

"Aye, the fossils, He put there," the minister said. "The Flying Spaghetti Monster put them there Himself, giving the scientists something to dig up. And why did He do this?"

Jezzie yelled out "To test our faith!"

"Aye," the minister nodded in approval. "That be correct! The Flying Spaghetti Monster wants to test our faith! The fossils haven't been there for millions of years. No! The Flying Spaghetti Monster just put them there a few thousand years ago."

"A few thousand years ago!" the pirate wench echoed.

"And what of the measurements that scientists make?" the minister asked. "They date the carbon, do they not? Ha! Date the carbon!"

"Scientists date carbon!" the pirate wench said with a shrill mocking laugh.

"Aye, and how be it that scientists believe fossils are millions of years old when they truly be only a few thousand years old?" the minister asked.

"Because the Flying Spaghetti Monster alters their measurements with His Noodly Appendage!" Jezzie shouted out.

"Aye," the minister said. "He reaches down with His Noodly Appendage and He changes the measurements. Ye cannot trust yer eyes! Ye cannot trust yer tests! And why does His Noodliness do this?"

"To test our faith!" they all answered.

"Aye! He alters things to appear to be what they do not be, and He does this to test our faith. But ye all have faith, do ye not?" the minister said. "Ye all have been touched by His Noodly Appendage. I can see it in yer eyes. I can see it from the holy colanders ye wear upon yer heads. But how do ye show yer faith?"

"How do you show your faith?" the pirate wench echoed.

"By dressing like a pirate!" said the young man with the fake eye patch.

"By wearing colanders on our heads," said the woman with the beaded belt.

"Aye, aye, me mateys," the minister said. "Those all be good ways to show yer faith in His Grand Noodliness. But ye are in luck today for ye have an extra special chance to show yer faith. Right now in the room next door there be a decision being made. Will we follow the Flying Spaghetti Monster? Will we acknowledge the work of His Noodly Appendage? That be the question before us in the room next door. That be the chance ye have to show yer faith! So get ye next door. Go on, get ye next door!"

The minister waved his hands, trying to shoo them out of the room. Kale was the first to jump to his feet. He hadn't expected a room change and, being so hungry, he didn't relish the idea of moving much, but if they found seats in a different room, that gave him a chance to grab a chair on Jezzie's right instead of her left and thereby avoid her snotty elbow.

"We'd better go," he said, trying to speak with the self-confidence he imagined came naturally to pickup artist heroes like AlphaAlphaInfinity; and to his amazement, Jezzie actually stood up and followed him toward the door. The other Pastafarians, however, moved in the opposite direction, crowding around the Pastafarian minister and bombarding him with questions. The minister began answering them passionately but Kale and Jezzie were already in the hallway and didn't hear the discussion.

"Isn't it awesome?" Jezzie said. "I told you, everything religious people believe without proof can just as easily have been done by the Flying Spaghetti Monster. That's how you know it's a religious belief instead of a scientific one! Take Intelligent Design for example. Believers claim it's a scientific theory, but it has no more proof than the Flying Spaghetti Monster, which means it's actually a religious belief!"

Kale nodded his head absently, eager to get Jezzie sitting down next to him and to move forward with his pickup artist techniques. Maybe a good neg would come to him if he thought hard enough.

The room next door proved to be room 5a, where a school board meeting was taking place according to the glass-covered bulletin board next to the door. Kale opened the door and went in, Jezzie following behind. It was much the same as the other room, the same old tile floor, the same miscellaneous posters on the walls. But the chairs here were metal folding chairs rather than orange plastic ones, and they had been organized into rows, the seats half-filled with people. The chairs all faced the front of the room, where there was a wooden table with five people sitting behind it, a single microphone in the center of the table. A propped-up folded piece of paper declared the man sitting in the center of the table to be the school board president. He had dark brown skin, closely shaved hair, and thick glasses with black rims. Sitting on both sides of him, two on each side, were a pair of graying men and women, all with caucasian skin and unreadable expressions on their faces. Those must be the school board members.

"What do you think is going on?" Kale asked Jezzie quietly as they walked toward the back row.

"I don't know," she whispered in return. "Maybe they're trying to put Intelligent Design in their science curriculum or something like that. Maybe that's why the Pastafarian minister wanted us to come here, so we could stop them from imposing their religious beliefs onto a public school."

Between the audience and the school board, there were two microphones, which faced the school board, where members of the public could stand and speak. There were two men at the microphones right now. The one nearest to Kale and Jezzie was a chubby man with caucasian skin, his brown hair long and pulled back in a ponytail. He appeared to be in his late forties and wore a rainbow shirt above black dress pants. The other man had the same skin tone and hair color but looked a few years younger and was sporting a goatee. He wore a button-up shirt, tucked into blue jeans, his outfit revealing a fairly standard dad bod.

The man with the goatee was speaking, alternating his attention between the man with the ponytail and the school board sitting behind the table. "These are existing words that already have a meaning," he said, "yet we're supposed to change that meaning just because you say so? And what's worse, even though the meaning of the word has completely changed, we're supposed to keep using it the same way we did before you changed its meaning?"

The last two rows of seats were empty. Kale hurried and sat on the second seat of the back row, leaving the end seat open. He gestured for Jezzie to sit down next to him, congratulating himself on perfectly positioning himself to progress with the touching technique. Now her snot-contaminated elbow would be safely away from him on the other side of her body.

Goatee man continued, the frustration heavy in his voice. "It's like you took a Coke bottle, poured Pepsi inside, and then demanded that Coke lovers still love the drink, despite what's inside, because the bottle still says 'Coke' on the label."

Jezzie sat down and Kale began to plan his angle of attack. He had to be subtle, but it had to also be noticeable enough to start increasing her attraction to him. The pickup artists in the forums made it seem so easy, but here in the real world sitting next to a real woman, it didn't seem so easy at all.

" 'Man' and 'woman' are real words with real meanings," goatee man said. "They aren't just made-up words you can change the definition of because you feel like it."

Ponytail man rolled his eyes and spoke with a condescending tone. "We've already gone over this. Gender is a social construct."

"Says who?" goatee man said. "Are urinals a social construct too? Why do we put urinals in boys' bathrooms but not in girls' bathrooms? Or should we change that too?" He threw his hands up in the air in exasperation.

This man was clearly upset. "Let's do it! A bathroom with nothing but urinals from wall to wall, and then we'll say it's a girls' bathroom. Why not? Gender is a social construct, right? So what if we just poured Pepsi into that bottle, the label says 'Coke', and that means it's Coke! Drink it up! It's Coke! It's all just a social construct, right?" He was practically shouting into the microphone, electronic feedback from the speakers overpowering the end of his sentence.

The school board president leaned toward the microphone on the table in front of him. "Sir, I'm going to have to ask you to calm down. This is the public comment period for our decision about the school district's bathroom policies. You have been given permission to share your opinion with the school board, but if you cannot keep your comments civil, you will be removed from this meeting."

Jezzie was sitting with her arms folded. Kale still wanted to go for her elbow since that seemed like the safest target and he had gone to such trouble to sit on the non-snotty side of her, but the angle of her arms made it a little awkward. He pulled his left arm back, ready to bring his hand forward and "accidentally" brush her elbow. His stomach fluttered, with nervousness this time instead of hunger.

Goatee man paused for a moment to compose himself. "I'm sorry," he said, looking at the school board president. "You're right. Being angry isn't helpful. I'll calm down. But you've got to understand ... you see ... I'm a religious man—"

"That's no surprise," ponytail man said, using the same condescending tone as before. "But public school policies cannot be based on religious beliefs."

"But that's my whole point," goatee man said. He

pointed a finger at ponytail man. "You're the one trying to impose religious beliefs on the school, not me."

Ponytail man laughed. "Don't be ridiculous. I'm an atheist. I don't believe in God, and I don't believe in Allah, and I don't believe in Odin either. I'm an atheist. I don't believe in any religion, which means I don't have any religious beliefs to impose on anyone."

"But you believe in gender identity," goatee man said. "You believe that a biological male, with XY chromosomes and a male anatomy, is a woman if he says he's a woman—if he identifies as a woman."

"What's your point?" ponytail man replied. "Gender is a social construct and it's determined largely by identity. That's not a religious belief."

"So it's scientific then?"

"Of course it is. Why else would an atheist like me believe it?"

"So it's based on empirical evidence?"

Jezzie's eyes lit up at the mention of "empirical evidence", and she leaned forward, the colander on her head almost falling off, as she rested her elbows on her knees. Kale cursed under his breath. There was no way for him to touch her elbow now without making it too obvious. He would have to change tactics.

"Well . . . " ponytail man said, his condescending tone gone, replaced by uncertainty.

"Russell's teapot," goatee man said. "You're an atheist—as you have repeatedly told us—surely, you've heard of it?" He paused for a moment before going on. "There's a small teapot orbiting in space between Earth and Mars. It's too small for our eyes to see, too small for our telescopes to see, but it's there. It's there because I say it's there."

Jezzie hit Kale's leg and gestured toward the man with the goatee. "This is what I was telling you about," she said. Kale thrilled at the physical contact. Didn't that mean she was starting to come on to him? He tried to remember what the pickup artists had said about it in the message forum.

Ponytail man seemed confused at what goatee man had said. "Yes, but Russell's teapot is an analogy that is used to deal with religious claims. If you make a claim that can't be disproven, then no one is obligated to believe it. It's your responsibility to prove it."

"Right," goatee man said, "So, tell me something: How can I prove that someone isn't a transgender?"

"What?" ponytail man spurted. "But that's ... that's not ... " He struggled for an answer. Then his eyes lit up. "Well, you can just ask them! It's based on their identity!"

"No, no, no, no, no, no, no," goatee man said. "I asked you for empirical evidence. I asked you for something I can see, something I can touch, something I can measure, something I can independently verify. That's science, isn't it? Objectivity. Repeatability. Isn't that what science is? Physical, observable reality. There are urinals in the boys' bathroom but not in the girls' bathroom. There is Coke in a Coke bottle. These are real words with real meaning in a real world. If you needed to know how tall someone was, you wouldn't just ask them what height they identified as, you'd measure their height. If you needed to know how heavy someone was, you wouldn't just ask them what weight they identified as, you'd measure their weight. And if you needed to know if there really was a teapot orbiting out in space, you wouldn't just believe someone who claimed it was there, you'd get out a telescope and find out for yourself. Real evidence. Objective evidence.

Empirical evidence. That's what science is. So let me ask you again. How can I prove, using empirical evidence, that someone isn't a transgender?"

Ponytail man answered softly. "You can't."

Goatee man spread his arms out wide. "I rest my case. Gender identity is a religious belief and it therefore should not be used as a basis for public school bathroom policies."

Ponytail man spoke excitedly. "It's not a religious belief! I told you: I'm an atheist! Gender is a combination of chromosomes, hormones, anatomy, and identity."

"Says who?" goatee man asked. "What reproducible test based on empirical evidence proved that identity should be included in that list?"

"He's right, you know," Jezzie whispered to Kale.

Kale was still racking his brain trying to remember if her hitting his leg like that should be interpreted as a come-on or not. But hearing Jezzie refer to a different guy sent warning bells off in Kale's head. He knew it wasn't good if her attention was on someone else instead of on him and his game.

"You think you're so smart," ponytail man said to goatee man. "You think you're so clever. Well, what about the intersex then? A person can have XY chromosomes and female anatomy. Explain that! That proves that gender isn't just based on chromosomes."

"Yes, you're right," goatee man began.

"Ha!" ponytail man said. "I told you: I'm an atheist. Accusing me of believing a religious belief ... How ridiculous."

"I wasn't finished," goatee man said. "You're right that there are birth defects that cause physical ambiguity about what gender a person is, biological anomalies where chromosomes and body parts don't line up like they should, causing actual, physical, observable ambiguity between the two genders. Thankfully this is rare, like other birth defects, but here's the key point: You can prove that someone is intersex, and more importantly, you can prove that someone isn't intersex. People aren't intersex because they identify as intersex. They are intersex because they actually are intersex, because there is actual, real, provable ambiguity in their physical bodies."

"But there is ambiguity in transgender bodies as well," ponytail man said. "Their physical bodies are one gender, but they identify as another."

"And there's a small teapot orbiting out in space. That's my claim. I can't prove it. I have no empirical evidence, nothing you can measure, no way for you to prove me right or prove me wrong, so I guess that means you just have to believe what I say, right?" goatee man said. "Wrong. That's not how science works."

Jezzie gestured at the goatee man, whispering to Kale, "This is what I was telling you about earlier. You can't just say something and expect people to believe it with no proof. That's not how science works!"

Kale glared at the man with the goatee. This stupid man with this stupid facial hair making his stupid points. Jezzie's attention was all focused on what goatee man was saying. None of Kale's pickup artist techniques would work if Jezzie wasn't paying attention to him! Kale wondered what AlphaAlphaInfinity would do in this situation. Something alpha-like certainly, but what?

"I told you earlier that I'm a religious man," goatee man went on, looking at ponytail man. "But that doesn't mean I don't also believe in science. These are two separate things, religion and science, each providing two separate reasons to believe. I believe things for scientific reasons because they can be proven to me. I believe things for religious reasons because I choose to believe them. When you argue on behalf of gender identity, you're using a religious argument. You aren't proving to me that a biological man is a woman. You're telling me that he says he is a woman and therefore I should believe him. That's a religious argument. And I don't choose to believe it."

"It isn't a religious argument," ponytail man said. "Am I referring to God? Am I referring to scripture? Am I invoking some authority you have to believe because they are an authority? No!"

"Who says religion requires a god or scriptures?" goatee man said. "You are asking us to have faith in some unseeable, unknowable, unprovable identity, not something we ourselves can prove, not something we ourselves can ever objectively know. You are asking us to take it on faith, not proof. What else would that be besides religion? I'm a religious man. I understand the difference between scientific facts and religious beliefs, and I'm telling you that gender identity is a religious belief."

"That's ridiculous," ponytail man said.

"Is it?" goatee man said. "Religious beliefs are believed to be true because they are believed to be true, not because they have been scientifically proven. They have been placed outside of scientific inquiry. We believe a religious belief because we choose to believe it. Is there proof for resurrection? Yet some people choose to believe in it. Is there proof for reincarnation? Yet some people choose to believe in it. Is there proof for gender identity? Yet you choose to believe in it. You choose to believe the religious belief of gender identity the same way other people choose to believe in resurrection or reincarnation."

"It's ridiculous to claim that gender identity has no

proof," ponytail man said. "There have been multiple brain scan studies that show a statistical correlation among people who identify with a different gender than their cisgender."

Jezzie leaned toward Kale. "What's cisgender?" she whispered. Kale had no idea, but he was thrilled to have her attention back on him and even more thrilled that she had just walked into a perfect neg he could use on her.

"What? You mean you don't know? I thought everyone knew that," Kale said. He was pleased with himself. Now he could get things back on track! Except the insult didn't seem to make her more attracted to him like it was supposed to. She just glared at him and then turned back to the two men arguing in front of the school board. Dealing with real women was hard!

"Cisgender, you mean biological gender, right?" goatee man said.

"Right. The studies—the scientific studies!—show a correlation in the brains of those who identify with a gender different from their cisgender," ponytail man said, smirking.

"A correlation?"

"That's right."

"A statistical correlation?"

"Exactly, and that's proof," ponytail man said. "Gender is more than just DNA. Gender is more than just anatomy. You wanted empirical evidence, and there you have it!"

Goatee man tilted his head, his lips raised in a slight smile, giving the impression that ponytail man had just made a profound mistake. "Empirical evidence, eh?" goatee man said. "But you told me earlier it wasn't possible to prove someone wasn't a transgender through empirical evidence?"

"What? No, that's not what we're talking about here," ponytail man said, trying to regain his rhetorical footing. "This isn't a way to prove someone isn't a transgender. This is just proof that gender identity is real—that it's scientific!"

"Okay," goatee man said. "First off, I fail to see why a diagnosis from brain scans would be used to trump physical reality. Schizophrenia has signs and symptoms that can be seen in brain scans as well, did you know that? Someday we might be able to diagnose it entirely through brain scans. And when that day comes, does that mean we'll stop trying to cure it? Will we expect everyone else to bend reality to the viewpoint of the person suffering from schizophrenia? Of course not. We won't bend physical reality to match their delusions, so why would we do that for those who reject the physical reality of their gender?"

"You asked me for proof and I provided proof!" ponytail man said. "Studies have shown that the brain scans of transgenders have similarities to the gender they identify with! That's proof!"

"Once again, you didn't let me finish," goatee man said. "So what you're saying is that everyone who claims to be transgender has had their brain scanned and it's been proven through their brain scans that they are transgender? Each and every one?"

"Well, no ... "

"And if someone identifies as a transgender, yet their brain lacks the correlations, the similarities, the whatever that you claim proves gender identity, then you would agree that that proves they aren't really transgender?"

Ponytail man squirmed in front of the microphone. "No, of course not. That's determined by their identity!"

"So, no matter what the brain scans say. If a biological man says 'I am a woman', you're going to believe him?"

"Yes, but brain scans are proof that gender identity is real!"

"Oh, please. Brain scans can't be proof if you don't accept them as disproof. That's not how science works!" goatee man said, shaking his head. "That isn't science. That's religious apologetics. Can people scientifically prove there was a worldwide flood? No, but they can find nuggets of scientific evidence here and there which, taken by themselves, can make those people comfortable with a belief that otherwise contradicts current scientific understanding when taken as a whole. Would those people ever allow their belief in a worldwide flood to be disproven by the evidence they claim proves them right? Of course not. Because they aren't really engaging in science, they are engaging in religious apologetics. They aren't trying to prove something, not scientifically at least—because to scientifically prove something puts you at risk of having it disproven instead. They're just trying to pick and choose the facts that justify the religious belief they've already chosen to believe."

Goatee man looked back and forth between ponytail man and the school board. "Don't get me wrong," he said. "I'm not saying that's a bad thing. It doesn't mean they're stupid, and it doesn't mean they're wrong, at least not in the 'once we know the truth of all things' religious sense. But it's not science either. Science and religion are different. And gender identity, as you have just demonstrated, is religion. You don't care about proof. You don't care about empirical evidence. DNA, physical anatomy, brain scans, all of those bow down to the magical words 'I am whatever gender I claim to be.' You just listen to what you're told, and you believe it. Because there's an unseeable teapot flying through space between Earth and Mars. You know it's true because someone told you it's true. And you're not going to give anyone a chance to prove you wrong!"

"You misunderstand me," ponytail man said, his face beginning to turn red. "The science of brain scans is still in its infancy. But if you look at the evidence so far, it's clear that one day we will be able to identify a transgender mind."

"So you say," goatee man said. "Just like every other religious person says. No one believes their religious beliefs are wrong. Everyone expects science to one day prove their religious beliefs to be right. You aren't unique in that regard. Perhaps that day actually will come for gender identity. I seriously doubt it, but perhaps it will. Either way, that day is not today. And until that day comes, gender identity remains a religious belief just like any other unfalsifiable, unprovable religious belief."

Ponytail man muttered something under his breath. His face was getting redder.

"Besides, even if that day did come," goatee man went on, "even if science one day proved gender identity through empirical evidence, what happens the next day when science, being science, reverses itself based on new evidence and once again provides no proof for gender identity? Would you reject gender identity at that point? Would you say, 'Well, science decided there is no proof, so I guess I won't believe it anymore.'? No, you wouldn't, just like you don't reject your belief in gender identity today despite its lack of scientific proof. You don't reject your belief in gender identity because your belief in gender identity is a religious belief, not a scientific one. You don't believe in gender identity because it has been scientifically proven to you. You believe in it because you choose to believe in it. Someone told you there is an unseeable teapot orbiting out there in space and, by golly, you believe them."

"I'm an atheist!" ponytail man said, face now bright red. "I'm not religious! Stop claiming I'm religious! You're the idiot who's religious! You said so yourself. You're the religious one! Any disagreement between us is because of your religious beliefs, not mine!"

Goatee man's eyes narrowed. "How convenient for you. And that's how you really see it, isn't it? You've grown so accustomed to always being on the secular side, the scientific side, of an argument that you can't even conceive that you might unknowingly have slipped into fighting for the religious side, and me, an openly religious man, fighting for the scientific side. Wow, the cognitive dissonance must be overwhelming you. You, a smug, arrogant atheist, suddenly realizing that you're arguing on behalf of an unseeable teapot you claim is orbiting out in space because someone told you it was."

"F— you!" Ponytail man exploded, spittle spraying down on his rainbow shirt.

Microphone static filled the room as the school board president broke into the conversation. "Let's calm down and keep this civil."

"Don't tone police me!" Ponytail man yelled at the school board president. "This is important, and when something's important, then civility can just f— off!"

"Enough!" the school board president said, his voice firm. "This is a public discussion on whether or not this district should permit its students to use the bathroom of the gender they identify with rather than the bathroom of their biological sex. You have been permitted to provide feedback on this decision, but as I stated at the beginning, those who cannot speak civilly will be asked to leave."

Ponytail man muttered, glaring at both the school board president and the man with the goatee, but he relented, pausing for a moment to compose himself, before speaking slowly. "I am not arguing for the religious side. I am an atheist. I fight for science! This is not something I just believe because I choose to believe it, like you keep saying. It's not some wacko theory that respectable people think is nuts. If you ask someone who is knowledgeable in the area, someone who is properly educated, someone who has expertise, they will tell you it is the truth. Gender identity is real! It is as real as DNA or anatomy. It is as real as this microphone I am speaking into right now. Just ask a psychologist. Go ahead and ask them! They will tell you that a person's gender identity is real and should be respected."

"That's what a psychologist would say, is it?" goatee man said, also speaking slowly. "How embarrassing for members of that profession. Gender identity is either a religious belief or it is a delusion. If psychologists are preaching gender identity, then either they have inverted the loony bin and admitted us all, allowing the inmates to run the asylum, or else their profession has warped into one of religious evangelism."

"It's not religion! You act as if the gender binary is some undeniable reality, but it's not! Other societies have recognized more than two genders before. There's the proof you are asking for!"

"Other societies have also believed in prophets, and oracles, and witches, and wizards," goatee man said. "Does that prove those are real too?"

Ponytail man looked dangerously close to dropping the f-bomb again. "Gender is not determined solely by DNA," he said. "Look at the case of the intersex. Their anatomy doesn't follow their chromosomes like you claim it should."

"Back to the intersex again?" Goatee man shook his head. "I agree that's a really crappy birth defect, but you're trying to treat the intersex condition like a Trojan horse. We let that condition through the door and deal with it since it's actually physically provable, and then suddenly you burst out of the Trojan horse and demand that we let people identify as whatever they want despite the complete lack of physical evidence. No, those are two completely different things. I already said this before: People aren't intersex because they identify as intersex. They are intersex because they actually are intersex. It's a real condition, in the real world, provable through real evidence. It's completely different from gender identity."

"But that doesn't mean you should insult people by claiming gender identity is just a religious belief."

"Why in the world would it be insulting to think of something as a religious belief?" goatee man said. "Look who you're talking to. Did you forget I told you I'm a religious man? It's not my fault if you have a condescending attitude toward religious people. That's your problem, not mine. I have no problem if people believe in things for religious reasons. Unlike you, I don't think that makes them stupid. I think openly religious people are just as smart as you are. Frankly, I think they're smarter. At least we understand the difference between science and religion. Science is shared through proof. Religion is shared through persuasion. You can't prove to me that a biological male is a woman, but you certainly can try to persuade me to believe it. Except, as I keep repeating, that would be religion, not science."

"You can't just claim that a secular belief is religious!"

ponytail man said.

"And you can't just claim that a religious belief is secular! You can't expect us to teach it in public schools. You can't expect us to base our bathroom policies on it. And gender identity is a religious belief," goatee man said. "If you can't prove that someone isn't a transgender, then you can't prove that someone is. Science demands a two-way street. If you find yourself on a one-way road where only supportive facts are allowed and all contradicting facts are ignored, then you've entered the realm of religion, where something is true because it's true, not because it's been objectively proven. There's nothing wrong with one-way roads like that—I'm a religious man myself, and I travel them when I choose to do so—but you need to be honest about what kind of road you're traveling on."

"Gender identity is supported by facts! It's supported by just as many facts as your beliefs about gender!"

"Oh, please." Goatee man rolled his eyes. He gestured at the people all around him. "Strip off everyone's clothes in this room, and I'll wager I can identify each and every person's gender. And I'll be able to do it using provable, repeatable, observable, measurable, falsifiable standards. Can you do that using gender identity?"

"Gender is a personal ... an intrinsic ... " ponytail man started to say before switching tactics. "I would never presume to dictate someone's gender to them! It's something they must determine on their own."

"Ah. So there is no test. There is no proof. This is nothing observable, nothing measurable."

"Of course there is. There is their identity! They can tell you what gender they are. That's the proof!"

"Ah, of course," goatee man said. "Their words. Such powerful words. Words more powerful than physical reality, evidently. They sound magical. Magical words. Magical, mystical words. Magical, mystical—religious—words."

"They are not religious words! A person's gender is their personal truth! Who are you to say what is someone else's personal truth?"

"Who am I? Who am I indeed. Who is anyone for that matter? How dare we tell someone they are 5' 8" when they identify as 6' 2". How dare we tell them they are 47 years old when they identify as 29."

"That's completely different," ponytail man said.

"So you say," goatee man said. "So you say." Then his eyes brightened and his lips showed a slight smile. "Identity is so powerful for you, isn't it? Your world revolves around it, doesn't it? Well, tell me something, are you familiar with the beliefs of The Church of Jesus Christ of Latter-day Saints?"

"No, and I don't see why that's relevant," ponytail man said.

"They're often called 'Mormons'. Are you familiar with their beliefs?" goatee man asked.

"I've seen the play," ponytail man said, dismissively.

"They believe the president of their church is a prophet, a modern-day Moses, did you know that? And he believes that about himself as well. He identifies as a prophet. So tell me: Do you have to accept his identity? Do you have to believe his personal truth that he is a prophet?"

"Well ... that is ... well ..."

"He's caught him now," Jezzie whispered to Kale. Kale just wished both men would shut up and stop ruining his game. His stomach wouldn't stop rumbling. Stupid Pastafarians and their stupid meetups without food.

"Be careful here," goatee man said to ponytail man. "Keep in mind there are real consequences to your decision.

The word 'prophet' is a real word with a real meaning—just like the words 'man' and 'woman' are real words with real meanings. If someone is a prophet, then their words are authoritative. A prophet speaks for God. So suddenly any pronouncements they make about the meaning of life—or about sin—have to be taken seriously because they are a prophet. So let's be clear about the consequences to my question. Now tell me, do you accept his identity as a prophet with all the consequences that word entails? Or do you reject his identity?"

Ponytail man waved a hand dismissively. "That's not what we're talking about here."

"That's exactly what we're talking about here," goatee man said. "You're privileging identity over everything else—over proof, over physical reality itself. I am merely showing you the consequences of your point of view."

"But that's completely irrelevant. We're talking about gender here, which is nothing more than a social construct."

"So the only time that identity trumps reality, the only time out of everything in the world, is with gender?"

"Exactly, because gender is just a social construct."

"Who gave you the right to declare that gender, out of everything else, should be based on identity when everything else should not?" goatee man said. Then he added, "Perhaps it's you that is the prophet."

"I'm not claiming to be a prophet!"

"No? Yet you decided that with gender—and only with gender—magical words can overrule physical reality itself. What gives you the right to make that declaration? Who do you think you are? God?"

"Blasphemy!" The whole room shook with the angry cry, and Kale almost jumped out of his seat in surprise. Everyone turned and looked at the back of the room, where the Pastafarian minister, his pirate wench, and the rest of the Pastafarians all stood by the open door. The Pastafarian minister was glaring at the goatee man, his eyes filled with white-hot fire. "There be only one God," the minister said, his words slow and hard, "and He be composed of a clump of spaghetti with willowy eyestalks and two large meatballs!"

Goatee man looked at the Pastafarian minister in his pirate garb and at the pirate wench and at the other Pastafarians standing beside them wearing less enthusiastic renditions of pirate apparel. "What is this," he asked, "some sort of pirate fetish cosplay convention? And what are you all wearing on your heads?"

The Pastafarian minister strode further into the room, raising an accusing finger at the goatee man. "This landlubber hath committed blasphemy!" he yelled. "Seize him!"

The Pastafarians in the back of the room all surged forward, their faces grim. They grabbed goatee man by both arms.

"And what do we do to blasphemers?" the pirate wench asked, looking devotedly at the Pastafarian minister, who smiled darkly, his tricorn hat tilted down and casting a shadow over his face. "We make them walk the plank," he said.

"Ha, ha," goatee man said, struggling against the Pastafarians holding his arms. "Very funny. But this isn't a ship, and in case you didn't notice, we're in the middle of a discussion."

The Pastafarians started dragging him toward the far wall. "Wait," goatee man said. "What are you doing? Are you serious? There isn't even a plank here!"

"Aye," the Pastafarian minister said, his dark smile not

showing in his eyes. "But there be a window!"

"What are you doing? Stop it!" Goatee man struggled, but there were Pastafarians dragging him by both arms and Pastafarians pushing him from behind. "This is a public meeting," he said. "I have a right to share my opinion. What are you doing?" The Pastafarian with the plastic eye patch opened the window and then, with a heave-ho, they all tossed goatee man out the window. Then the Pastafarian with the plastic eye patch slammed the window shut and they all turned back to their minister, as if awaiting further instructions.

"Did they seriously just do that?" Jezzie whispered to Kale, a look of disbelief on her face.

"I know," Kale said. "These guys are awesome, aren't they?"

"Are you kidding me?" Jezzie asked, looking between Kale and the Pastafarian minister, who was now hobbling to the front of the room, his peg leg clunking with each step. When he reached the two microphones, he shoved ponytail man out of the way. Ponytail man didn't argue. He just meekly sat down in the front row.

The school board president stood up. "What is the meaning of this? This is a public meeting. You can't come in here and throw people out and push people around! Do you want us to call the police?"

But the school board member to his right reached up and grabbed his elbow. "Let's hear what he has to say."

Kale thought that was a wonderful idea. Jezzie loved this Pastafarian crap. She loved making fun of religious people and their willingness to believe things without proof. The more the Pastafarian minister talked, the happier she was and the better his chances, he figured.

The school board president eyed the Pastafarian minister warily.

"This is a public discussion," another school board member said. "We let those other two share their opinions. Surely we can allow some time to hear what this pirate thinks about it?"

It seemed odd to have a school board member refer to the Pastafarian minister like that, but Kale didn't care since it got him what he wanted. The remaining two members of the school board voiced agreement that they wanted to give "the pirate" his turn to speak, and the school board president relented. "Alright," he said, sitting down, "but no more roughness out of you," he said to the minister, "do you understand me?"

"Aye, Captain," the minister said, winking at the school board members.

The pirate wench came and stood in front of a microphone, and the Pastafarian minister started to pace back and forth, his peg leg clunking impressively on the tile floor with each step as he divided his attention between the audience and the school board.

"I see there be few here who be wearing the holy colander on yer heads, so there be many here who be needing to learn about yer Noodly Creator, the Flying Spaghetti Monster."

The minister stopped pacing for a moment to rest a hand on his chest. "I, yer humble pirate, be an ordained minister of His Noodliness." He reached into his pocket and unfolded his printed ordination certificate, holding it high for the crowd to see. "Which makes me qualified to preach to ye all and to teach ye of the truth."

"The truth!" his pirate wench echoed.

"Aye, me wench, I will teach ye all the truth," the minister said, placing his certificate back in his pocket and starting to pace again. "Do ye know of the Flying Spaghetti Monster? Have ye heard of His Noodliness? He be a mass of noodles with two large meatballs and two eyestalks, floating here, floating there, floating who knows where. And have ye seen him?"

"Have ye seen him?" the pirate wench echoed.

"No," the minister shook his head. "No, ye cannot. For He be invisible! Ye cannot see Him but ye know He be there because ye can see the effects of His Noodly Appendage!"

"Effects!" the pirate wench said. "Noodly Appendage!"

"Aye, our Noodly Creator created the earth. He created the land and the sea. And we be His creatures, for He created us too, starting with a midget."

"A midget!" the pirate wench echoed.

"Aye, our Noodly Creator be a good god," the minister went on. "There be a beer volcano and a stripper factory in heaven. Everything a pirate be needing to be happy."

"A stripper factory in heaven!" the pirate wench said.

"But here on Earth He tests us," the minister said. "He put fossils in the ground. And every time a scientist makes a measurement to test the age of the Earth, the Flying Spaghetti Monster alters it with His Noodly Appendage. And why does He do that?"

"Why does He do that?" the pirate wench echoed, looking at the audience.

"To test our faith!" the minister answered. "We need to show our faith in the Flying Spaghetti Monster. We need to show our faith in His Noodly Appendage. Evidence, measurements, physical reality—pshaw!"

"He tests our faith!" the pirate wench said.

"Aye, me buxom wench, aye. His Noodliness do be testing our faith. And not just about creation. No, His Noodly Appendage be altering and changing and hiding—

many things, many, many things."

"His Noodly Appendage!" the pirate wench said.

"And that be the reason why I be standing before ye today, me mateys. I, yer humble pirate, yer ordained minister of the Pastafarian religion, I be here because ye have a choice to make. Will ye follow yer weak human minds, or will ye show yer faith in the Flying Spaghetti Monster?"

"Will you show your faith!" the pirate wench said.

"Aye, and let me tell ye about yer faith," the minister said. "Supposing ye be a lassie. Supposing ye be, aye? And supposing ye be showering in the girls' locker room, aye? And supposing a matey of yers comes into the girls' shower, and supposing ye look down yonder and see that yer matey has a pe—"

The school board president cleared his voice loudly in the microphone. "I will have to ask you to avoid such language please," he said.

The Pastafarian minister paused his pacing and eyed the school board president, a flash of anger flaring on his face but quickly passing. "Arr ..." he said. "Very well. Very well. Supposing," he said, resuming his pacing, "supposing ye look down and this matey of yers, who just be entering the girls' shower, supposing ye see that yer matey has boy parts down yonder."

"Boy parts!" the pirate wench said.

"Aye, supposing that be what ye see," the Pastafarian minister said. "What would ye do? Would ye scream like a ninny? Would ye shout and say there be a lad in the girls' bathroom?" He shook his head. "No, I be hoping ye wouldn't be doing that. For that not be a lad, me mateys. For if yer matey be a lad, why would he be going in the girls' shower?"

"She," the pirate wench corrected him.

The Pastafarian minister looked at her, confused at her interruption. Then he shrugged and went on. "Aye, me mateys, that be no lad, that be a lassie. Remember, me mateys, the Flying Spaghetti Monster always be testing yer faith! And remember, me mateys, His Noodliness tests yer faith by altering things with His Noodly Appendage. Ye cannot see it—for He be invisible. But ye can know it be there because ye have been told it be there. And so when ye look down and see yer matey has boy parts, ye should be knowing that the Flying Spaghetti monster be reaching into yer eyes with his Noodly Appendage, and He be tweaking yer corneas and He be twisting yer pupils and He be making ye see what no be there. Yer matey has no boy parts. Pshaw! Yer matey be a lassie and a lassie no be having no boy parts!"

"Girls have no boy parts!" the pirate wench said.

"Aye, me wench," the Pastafarian minister said. "Aye. So, those boy parts must not really be there! It must be the Flying Spaghetti Monster. He be testing yer faith. And ye need to show yer faith. Ye need to call yer matey a lassie. Ignore what yer eyes see. Show yer faith in the Flying Spaghetti Monster. Show yer faith!"

"Show your faith!" the pirate wench echoed.

"Aye, show yer faith," the minister said. He paced across the room, his peg leg clunking on the floor, everyone waiting in anticipation for his next words. "And how be it," the minister went on, "that yer matey knows he be a lassie?"

"She," the pirate wench interrupted him.

But the minister didn't appear to have heard her. He just kept on preaching. "When yer matey looks down, there be boy parts, so how be it yer matey knows he be a lassie?"

"She," the pirate wench said again.

The minister ignored his wench. "Because yer matey has faith in the Flying Spaghetti Monster! Yer matey knows of His Noodliness. Yer matey knows of the power of His Noodly Appendage. Yer matey knows the Flying Spaghetti Monster reaches down into our brains with His Noodly Appendage and touches us, telling us what gender we truly be. There be no reason to look down yonder," the minister said, gesturing at his crotch. "We only be needing to look up here," he pointed at his head. "We only be needing to listen to the Flying Spaghetti Monster, to let His Noodly Appendage touch us and tell us what gender we be!"

"The Flying Spaghetti Monster will touch us with His Noodly Appendage and tell us what gender we are!" the pirate wench said.

"What nonsense," Jezzie whispered to herself, barely loud enough for Kale to hear. "It wasn't supposed to be like this. It was supposed to be funny. No one was supposed to actually believe this crap!"

Kale wasn't sure what to make of that. She was the one that had dragged him here. This was her idea of a good time. Apparently it wasn't turning out how she had expected?

"Can ye understand?" the Pastafarian minister said as he started to pace in front of the room again. He looked from the school board to the audience. "Can ye see ye are being tested? Or do ye be needing to hear one more example?"

"One more example!" the pirate wench said excitedly.

"Arr ... very well," the minister said. "Supposing ye be a lad and there be a school dance approaching. Girls'

Choice. And supposing one of yer mateys asks ye to go to the dance, but supposing when ye look at yer matey, yer eyes tell ye yer matey is another lad like ye, supposing that all be true. Well remember, me mateys, the Flying Spaghetti Monster be testing ye! His Noodliness wants to see if ye have faith! Yer matey don't be no lad. No, he be a lassie."

"She" the pirate wench corrected him.

The Pastafarian minister looked at her. "It be a lad that was asked to the dance."

"Yes, but it was a girl that asked him," the pirate wench said.

"Aye," the minister said, "and ye can't see that yer matey be a lassie because the Flying Spaghetti Monster has touched ye with His Noodly Appendage. Yer eyes have gone bonkers. They be seeing stuff that no be there and not seeing stuff that be there. But ye need to have faith! The Flying Spaghetti Monster be a loving deity, He shows great favor to every man who shows faith in Him. There be a stripper factory in heaven, after all! So ye, being a lad who was just asked to the dance by a lassie who ye can't tell is a lassie, why ye, if ye have faith, can have confidence of two things." The minister paused to hold up two fingers. "One, ye can know that, no matter what yer eyes be telling ye, yer matey has girl parts, not boy parts. That be the truth, hidden by His Noodly Appendage. And two, owing to the great benevolence of His Noodly Goodness, which is shown to all men that be faithful, ye can know that not only does yer matey have girl parts, but he surely also has the most bountiful bosom ye ever be knowing."

"She," the pirate wench corrected him again.

"I told ye, me wench," the minister said, "it be a lad that was asked to the dance."

"Yes, but it was a girl that asked him," the pirate wench repeated.

"Aye," the minister said, "and one with a most bountiful bosom, ye can be sure. Arr ... ye can't see them, and ye can't feel them—thanks be to the mysterious and mischievous workings of His Noodly Appendage—but they be there, and ye be needing to have faith. We all be needing to have faith. Faith in the Flying Spaghetti Monster! Faith in His Noodly Goodness!"

The Pastafarians in the room all broke out in a cheer.

"What a load," Jezzie muttered. She took the colander off her head and set it on her lap.

Kale wasn't sure how to react. Why had she taken her colander off her head? Wasn't she into this stuff any more? Should Kale not be into it either? Or would it be bad for him to change what he liked just because she had changed what she liked? It certainly didn't seem like a very alpha thing to do. He wondered what AlphaAlphaInfinity would have to say about it.

The minister was still preaching, talking about the glories of the Flying Spaghetti Monster and His Noodly Appendages. It was all becoming quite repetitive at this point. The Flying Spaghetti Monster likes to test us. We need to have faith in Him. We need to trust in the Flying Spaghetti Monster instead of our own eyes. Any tests or measurements we might do are worthless because the Flying Spaghetti Monster likes to mess around with things. That was the gist of it all, repeated over and over again.

"What if there's an unseeable teapot orbiting out in space?" Jezzie suddenly shouted out, shocking Kale and the rest of the room with her outburst.

The minister didn't even miss a beat in his preaching. "Then the Flying Spaghetti Monster put it there!" he said, raising his hands high above his head in excitement. "And it be held in orbit by His Noodly Appendages, just like the planets be. And if ye be touched by His Noodly Appendage, ye can know if it be there or not. Ye don't need yer eyes. Ye don't need yer tests. Ye only need yer faith in the Flying Spaghetti Monster! Then ye can know, me mateys!"

Jezzie swore under her breath and shook her head. "I can't believe I wasted a night for this," she muttered.

Kale needed to show his alphaness. He needed to show he wasn't some weak "nice guy" that would just follow a woman around like some loser, liking whatever she liked, disliking whatever she disliked. That was the Kale of the past, but Kale was a new man now. The pickup artist message forum had shown him the way. "I think it's great," he lied, putting as much confidence into his voice as he could fake.

Jezzie glared at him.

"The choice be simple," the minister said, now facing the school board, his tricorn hat leaning dangerously over his eye patch. "Do ye want to be slaves to the wiles of naturalism? Do ye want to follow what ye can see or ye can measure like ye be faithless fools, or do ye want to show yer faith in the Flying Spaghetti Monster!"

The room fell silent. No one sure what to say. Finally, the school board president spoke. "Thank you, Mr ... er ... Pirate," he said. "I believe we have solicited sufficient feedback from the public, do you all agree?"

The four school board members all nodded.

"Alright," the school board president said, then he lowered his voice into a more formal tone, "A proposal has been brought before this school board to allow admittance into the girls' or boys' bathrooms based on a student's gender identity rather than their biological sex. This proposal will now be voted on by this school board, and their decision will take effect immediately. All those in favor of this proposal?"

The audience looked at the school board in anticipation, no one making a sound. The four school board members shared a glance with each other and then broke out into smiles. Simultaneously they reached beneath their seats and picked up a colander and placed it on their heads. Then they all raised their right hands, banging their left hands on the table. "Aye, Aye, Captain!"

The Pastafarian minister nodded vigorously in approval, the pirate wench clapped in excitement, and all the Pastafarians in the audience let out a huge cheer.

"What a load of BS," Jezzie said. She turned angrily to Kale. "You can keep this stupid thing," she said, shoving her colander in his lap. Then she hurried out of the room. Kale watched her leave, wanting to follow her but knowing it wouldn't be a very alpha thing to do. He was supposed to convince women to follow him, not the other way around! So he sat there all alone, trying desperately to look manly, wearing a colander on his head.

There Can Be No Demigods in Secularism

[This essay was written in March 2022, before Justice Jackson was confirmed as a Supreme Court Justice.]

The confirmation hearings for Judge Ketanji Brown Jackson to the United States Supreme Court recently had the following disturbing exchange:

Senator Blackburn: Can you provide a definition for the word 'woman'?

Judge Jackson: Can I provide a definition?

Senator Blackburn: Yeah.

Judge Jackson: I can't.

Senator Blackburn: You can't?

Judge Jackson: Not in this context. I'm not a biologist.

Keep in mind that unless there is a major surprise, Judge Jackson is going to be the next Supreme Court justice, one of the most powerful people of our nation, and this judge who is soon to be granted enormous power, and who will at times be deciding cases based on the reality of whether or not someone is a woman, is unwilling to say what a woman actually is.

Very unsettling.

The next day, Senator Cruz returned to this topic, and Judge Jackson said the following:

"Senator, I know that I am a woman. I know that Senator Blackburn is a woman, and the woman who I admire most in the world is in the room today, my mother."

Now, one might ask how it is that Judge Jackson knows she is a woman if she can't even define what a woman is, but one doesn't need to ask that question because we all know that Judge Jackson knows exactly what a woman is, just like I know what a woman is, just like you know what a woman is, just like everyone knows what a woman is — because women are actually part of secular reality. Women are adult human females. Or, to put it a different way, women are those whose physical biology proves they are a woman. If the sun fizzled out tomorrow, and the Earth froze over, and a million years in the future an alien race discovered our planet and dug us out of the ice, they would have no problem identifying who was a woman and who was a man — because the concept is based on proof, and they would have the same access to proof that we do today.

But there's been a recent complication ...

Now, we have women who are women because they can prove they are women, and we also have people who claim to be women even though they cannot prove they actually are. In fact, it's worse than that. They are claiming to be women, even though the physical evidence proves they are men. But they *believe* they are women. They *self-identify* as women. And we have been told we have to believe them. We have been told we have to discard the physical evidence and instead rely on faith in their words.

And a (very likely) future Supreme Court justice is

publicly showing homage to this demand of faith-based belief. Very unsettling indeed. If those who have been vested with the power to protect our secular nation have decided they don't want secularism anymore, what are we to do?

But this isn't the only recent example of the failure of our secular elite to protect secularism. In the news, you can read that Governor Cox of Utah recently vetoed a bill that would prevent boys who believe they are girls from playing in girls sports.

Now, let me say I do have sympathy for Governor Cox about this. I read his letter. I understand some of the process issues with the law, and some of the concerns about litigation. And also let me say that I have mixed feelings about laws like this. Yes, I understand the issue they are trying to solve, and it is an issue that absolutely does need to be solved, but laws like this are flawed because they are targeting just one effect of the problem instead of the problem itself. The actual problem which our government should be trying to resolve is that gender identity, a faith-based belief, is being treated as if it were a part of secular reality, but it is **not**.

And so yes, I do have some sympathy for Governor Cox's reasoning, yet from his letter it is clear that he, like so many of our secular elites, completely misunderstands the situation. I don't doubt his compassion for others, and I don't doubt that his compassion is a large part of how he approaches this topic, but compassion does not grant him rights that he does not have; and in a secular society, he has no right to demand that people accept a truth claim he cannot prove is true, and neither he, nor anyone else, can prove that a biological male is a woman.

Gender identity is based entirely on self-identity. It

is completely faith-based. We are told that people are whatever gender they tell us they are, and we are expected to simply believe them. All based on faith.

But that's not how secular reality works. A secular identity is not something we self-identify as. A secular identity is something that the physical evidence tells us about ourself. If you ask me how much I weigh, I don't tell you what weight I self-identify as, I tell you what weight the scale tells me I am — because my weight, like my height, like my age, like my racial heritage, like my biological sex (i.e. gender), are part of secular reality.

(As an aside: If anyone reading this is foolishly muttering under your breath, "gender is different than sex!", then you need to stop your deceptive nonsense right now. Believers in gender identity are absurdly unwilling (or unable) to provide their definition for the word "woman", but if you look at how they use the word, then the most honest and concise definition is obviously: "A woman is someone who identifies as a female." So, on the one hand, you claim "gender is different than sex", but then on the other hand you purposefully tie gender together with sex in how you use the words "man" and "woman". Your argument is dishonest and utter nonsense. That is all I will say about that.)

Now, let me clarify that when I speak of "secular reality" I am not talking about what ultimately is *true*. I am a religious man. I actually belong to the same religion as Governor Cox. I believe in God, I believe in Jesus Christ, I believe in the Bible, the Book of Mormon, and in prophets both ancient and modern. Those are just some of my faith-based beliefs, things I believe in even though I cannot prove to others that they are true.

But what if you don't believe in my faith-based beliefs?

What if you believe in entirely different faith-based beliefs? (And let me be clear, **everyone** has faith-based beliefs.) How are we supposed to function in a society if we can't even agree on what reality actually is?

The answer in history, unfortunately, has been that the powerful would rule over the weak, and faith-based beliefs would be imposed by force. Reality would be whatever the strong told you it was. Reality would be whatever Judge Jackson told you it was. Reality would be whatever Governor Cox told you it was. Is that the kind of society you want to live in, one where reality itself is dictated to you by the privileged few?

No, we're supposed to know better than that. We have been blessed by the Enlightenment. We have been blessed by the concept of secularism, by the idea that each of us can be equal, an idea that can only come to fruition through a single shared reality, not what we each individually believe is completely *true* but a handshake agreement we all make together that none of us have the right to impose our faith-based beliefs onto the other and therefore the shared secular reality we will interact within must be based on **proof**.

Let me be clear that religion operates in areas that secularism simply cannot reach because only religion (whether organized or informal) can provide us answers about things outside the realm of proof such as morality and the meaning of life. But when it comes to human civilization, secularism allows us to create a foundation of liberty and equality upon which a just and moral society can be developed — if we choose to do so.

And ultimately secularism is what is at risk here. We are the recipients of thousands of years of human history. We have been given the opportunity to stand on the shoulders of giants, to see further than any society has ever seen before. But we are currently stepping off that fortunate vantage point, finding ourselves in the same muck as countless prior generations, with reality once again being dictated to us by the privileged few.

Governor Cox mentioned a desire for compassion in his letter, and he emphasized the small number of individuals involved in the controversy in Utah when it comes to high school sports, making the point that with such a small number, shouldn't we err on the side of acceptance and kindness?

Well, let's make the example even more dramatic. Let's take the entire population of Utah. Based on the 2020 census, let's call that 3.2 million. Now, let's assume out of that population of 3.2 million that there is just one single man who believes he is a woman, just one. Now put yourself in this individual's shoes. Imagine the amount of anguish it would feel to believe, deep within your soul, that you are something that physical reality, and everyone around you, is constantly telling you you are not. Imagine how happier you would be if everyone else simply ignored physical reality and believed what you believed about yourself. And this is just one person, just one person out of a population of 3.2 million. So what's the big deal if we make just this one exception to secularism, just this one time?

Before you answer that, let's think through exactly what we're saying here. So we have a population of 3.2 million people. Each of those persons have their own faith-based beliefs, but because this is a secular society, those are not included in the shared secular reality. Except, that is, for this one individual's faith-based beliefs. Everyone else has to prove their truth claims, but not this person. This person can simply state a truth claim and automatically it becomes part of secular reality. Consider the power granted to that individual, power over reality itself. And what would you call such an individual? What would you call someone who has been bestowed with the power to dictate reality to everyone else? I would call them a demigod.

And so, could a population of 3.2 million mortals make space for one demigod? Perhaps. But such a society would no longer be a secular one — because there can be no demigods in secularism.

In his letter, Governor Cox spoke often of a desire for compromise. I am a member of Governor Cox's religion. I understand the motivation he feels for that compromise. But I am also a member of Governor Cox's secular nation, and secularism cannot tolerate any compromise that includes the presence of a faith-based belief within secular reality. That breaks the handshake agreement. That breaks secularism. And we return to the mistakes of the past, with reality dictated by the privileged few.

But a compromise actually is possible, a simple one in fact: Those who believe in gender identity need to codify their faith-based beliefs into an official religion, and then they need to request religious accommodation of their faith-based beliefs — just like the rest of us mortals. And they will be granted that religious accommodation, with the same compassion and fairness offered to all other religions.

Update: Ketanji Brown Jackson was sworn in as a Supreme Court justice on June 30, 2022.

On March 25, 2022, the Utah legislature rightfully overrode Governor Cox's veto, banning boys who believe they are girls from playing in girls' sports. To his credit, the following year after the Utah legislature passed a law banning gender-obscuring medical procedures for minors, Governor Cox signed it into law.

Unwanted Proof

Sara and Sally looked up from behind the receptionist desk as the door opened, and a middle-aged man entered the front lobby backwards, dragging a metal cart through the door, followed by a much younger redheaded woman, who was pushing the cart from behind.

The redheaded woman let the door close, and the middle-aged man turned to Sally and Sara as if to speak but froze when he saw them. Identical twins, Sara and Sally had the same lightly-tanned skin and blonde hair, although Sara wore it short and Sally wore it long. One wore blue and the other green, and the two women were both smiling at him with the kind of innocent expression that makes a good man feel guilty when he's attracted and a wise man remind himself to double-check IDs.

The redhead scowled and shoved the metal cart into the man's side. "Oof," he said. "Watch where you're going."

"I was," the redhead said. Pale caucasian skin, cheeks covered in freckles, her red hair drawn back in a lazy ponytail, she wore an oversized button-up shirt and jeans and looked to be in her mid-twenties.

"Welcome to Femina Laboratories," Sara said to the pair.

"Unfortunately we're closing," Sally said.

"We close at six," Sara said.

"And that's in ten minutes," Sally said.

The redhead looked down at her watch and grunted in frustration. "I told you we were late, Geoffrey," she said.

Geoffrey, the middle-aged man, waved her objections away. "And I told you it would be fine, Veronica." Geoffrey wore a plain t-shirt which hung loosely over dark jeans. He strode to the front desk and rested his hands on top of it. "I'd like to arrange third-party validation for an invention," he told the blonde receptionists.

"Okay," Sally said, "Unfortunately our Project Manager already left for the day."

"She had to pick up her kids," Sara said. "She always leaves early."

"But if you come back tomorrow morning, you could talk to her," Sally said.

"Tomorrow?" Geoffrey said. "You don't want me to come back tomorrow. You're going to want to see my invention right away. This is going to make Femina Laboratories famous!"

Sally and Sara rose in unison from their chairs and leaned forward to get a better look at the bulky contraption that lay atop the metal cart. It looked like an oddly shaped projector, with a glass lens on the front, a power cord and an on/off switch in the back. The only thing remarkable about it was that, because the middle was open, you could see a large red crystal that had been placed in the path of the machine's light.

"What is it?" Sara asked.

Geoffrey walked back and rested a hand on top of the machine proudly. "This," he said, "is proof of the unprovable."

Sara and Sally's eyes grew wide. "What can it prove?"

Geoffrey smiled at the twins, pausing for dramatic effect. "It can prove gender identity."

Sally and Sara sat down and looked up at Geoffrey expectantly.

"You know what gender identity is, don't you?" Geoffrey asked after an awkward moment.

Sara and Sally kept looking at him.

"Gender identity is where someone's gender is different from their biological sex. It's like where a man is a man physically, but he identifies as a woman, so he's actually a woman. That's what gender identity is."

Sara turned to Sally. "See, that's what Justine means when she talks about mansplaining."

Sally nodded. Then she said to Geoffrey, "Justine is our boss. She hates when men mansplain."

"Or talk," Sara said.

"Or breathe," Sally said.

"She hates pretty much everything about men," Sara said.

The two smiled sweetly up at Geoffrey again. "We know what gender identity is," Sara said. "One of our researchers is a man who identifies as a woman."

"Brooke is a woman," Sally said to Sara.

"Of course she is," Sara replied, her right eyebrow betraying a slight twitch.

Geoffrey appeared flustered. He looked to Veronica, who placed her hand on the machine beside his. "If you know what gender identity is, then you know it has no actual proof. Someone says they are a gender, and you are expected to just take their word for it. Until now." She patted the machine lightly. "This machine can show someone's gender identity."

Sally and Sara's eyes widened again. "How?" Sally

asked.

Veronica gestured at the opening on the side of the machine. "When you shine a light through the crimson crystal and illuminate someone, their gender identity becomes visible behind them."

Sara and Sally looked at each other, their mouths dropped open.

"That is so awesome!" Sara said.

"Can we see? Can we see?" Sally said, practically bouncing in her seat.

Geoffrey spread his hands in front of him. "That's what we're here for!" he said.

Sally looked at Sara. "We just cleared Lab C. Let's hook it up in there."

"Justine will be mad," Sara said. "It's almost 6 o'clock. We're supposed to be closing."

"But we can see someone's gender identity!" Sally said.

Sara smiled and nodded. The two stood and waved for Geoffrey and Veronica to follow them through the door behind the receptionist desk, which led into a long hallway. There was a room marked "Lab C", a few doors down. Geoffrey and Veronica wheeled the metal cart behind the twin blondes into Lab C, placed the machine in the center of the room, and then unwound the long extension cord and plugged it into an outlet on the wall.

"Okay," Geoffrey said. "Which one of you wants to go first?"

Sally and Sara looked at each other and they both shook their heads. They turned to Geoffrey.

"We don't want to go first," Sara said.

"It might fry our brains," Sally said.

Veronica snorted and rolled her eyes. "Would it make a difference?" she said softly to herself.

Sara and Sally both looked at Veronica.

"We heard that," Sally said.

"You have really pretty freckles," Sara said.

They smiled sweetly at her.

Veronica flushed bright red and dropped her eyes to study the floor.

With a soft squeal of wheels, a man wearing a blue jumpsuit walked past in the hallway pushing a mop and bucket.

Sally and Sara looked from each other to the hallway and then back at each other again.

Sara elbowed Sally. "You ask him," she said. "He likes you."

Sally elbowed Sara back. "No, you ask him," she said. "He likes you more."

"That's true," Sara said. Then she called out into the hallway. "Frantz, can you come in here for a second?"

The squeal of wheels in the hallway stopped, and a moment later the man in the blue jumpsuit appeared in the doorway. He was small, very small for a man, and half-bald, with deep-brown skin and tired eyes. A flashy crucifix dangled from his neck. "Yes?" he said to Sara in a thick accent, smiling wearily at her.

"Frantz, could you be a dear and go stand by that wall?" Sara said, pointing at the wall in front of the machine.

"The wall?" Frantz asked, confused.

"Yes, dear," Sally said. She walked over to Frantz and touched him lightly on the shoulder and then pointed with her other hand at the wall. "Over there, please."

"Pretty please," Sara added, her smile bright.

Frantz nodded slowly and trooped over to the wall. Then he turned around and looked back at the blonde twins as if to ask, "What now?"

"Turn it on," Sally, standing beside Sara once more, said to Geoffrey.

"Yes, turn it on," Sara said.

"Turn what on?" Frantz asked. But Geoffrey had already flipped the switch and light burst out of the machine. Frantz slammed his eyes shut and raised a hand to block the light, uttering a shocked curse.

The rest of the room was silent.

"Do you see it?" Geoffrey whispered in excitement. He turned back to Sara and Sally and spoke in a normal tone. "Do you see it?"

Sally and Sara's mouths hung open as they stared at Frantz. They turned to each other slowly and then exploded in unison.

"That is so awesome!" Sara said.

"So, so awesome!" Sally said.

The twins bounced up and down, hugging each other.

"It's his gender identity," Veronica said. Her blush was gone now and she spoke in an authoritative tone. "Do you see the light shade of blue? That means his gender identity is male."

"I see it," Sara said.

"I see it too," Sally said. "It's blue!" She smiled at Frantz across the room. "It's blue, Frantz!" she said. "That means you're a man!"

Frantz still had his hand raised in front of his face to block the light from the machine, but he peered from below his hand, looking from Sara to Sally in confusion. Geoffrey caught his eye and raised a finger, pointing behind him. Frantz slowly turned around and then jumped into the air, letting out a surprised squeak.

And the grayish-blue form behind Frantz leaped as well, matching his movement like a shadow—a three-dimensional shadow—cast from the machine. Frantz stared for a moment. Then he raised his hand, and the grayish-blue figure facing him raised a feature-less hand as well. Frantz looked back over his shoulder at Sara and Sally. He pointed at the grayish-blue figure. "It's my soul!" he said.

"Actually, it's your gender identity," Geoffrey said. "You can see that it's blue, which proves you're a man."

"You're a man, Frantz! You're a man!" Sally said. "It's that wonderful to know?"

"What does a woman's gender identity look like?" Sara asked Veronica and Geoffrey.

"It's pink," Veronica said.

"But how do you know it's actually Frantz's gender identity we're seeing?" Sara asked. "Frantz is a man anyway. What if we're just seeing his body?"

"We've tested it dozens of times on self-described transgenders," Geoffrey said. He flipped the switch and the machine's light turned off, the grayish-blue proof of Frantz's gender identity vanishing from the room. "The pink and blue follows their gender identity, not their biological sex," Geoffrey said. "It's 100% accurate. Never a single false result yet."

A series of sharp clicks began to sound down the hall, growing louder with each click. Sally and Sara looked at each other in excitement.

"You know who that is," Sara said.

"There's only one researcher who wears stiletto heels everyday to work." Sally said.

Then the two turned toward the hall, smiling in unison. "Brooke!" they shouted together.

The clicking came quicker, growing louder and louder until a large brunette appeared in the doorway. Wearing stilettos that showed off long shaved legs and a white lab coat that couldn't hide large shoulders and a prominent Adam's apple, Brooke smiled at the blonde twins. "Yes, sweeties? Did you need something? I was just fixing to leave. I gotta catch my train."

Sara hurried over to Brooke. "Come stand here for a moment," she said, dragging Brooke to the wall while Sally dragged Frantz back toward the hallway.

"Thanks, Frantz," Sally said as he left the room. "Isn't it nice to know you're a man?"

"What are y'all talking about?" Brooke asked. "Of course Frantz is a man. He's the only man that works here!"

"Just stand there," Sara said. Then she walked back to stand beside Sally behind the machine.

"Well, alright, sweetie," Brooke said, putting a hand on a hip and striking a pose. "How's this?"

"Turn it on!" Sally said, and Geoffrey flipped the switch.

Light burst from the machine once more. "Good heavens!" Brooke said, raising a manicured hand to block the light. "What are y'all trying to do? Blind me?"

"Look behind you!" Sara yelled. "Look behind you!"

Brooke turned to look and then almost tripped. "Oh my! What's that?"

Just like with Frantz, the light of the machine caused a grayish three-dimensional shadow to appear behind Brooke. But this one had a slight hint of pink to it.

"That's your gender identity," Veronica explained.

"It's pink," Brooke said.

"Because you're a woman!" Sara yelled.

"I'm a woman?" Brooke said, almost to herself. Then her voice rose in excitement. "Well, of course I'm a woman! That's what I've been telling y'all all this time. I'm a woman. I'm a woman!" She clapped her hands and hugged herself.

"Your biological sex is male, but your gender identity is female. And this proves it," Geoffrey said. "This is real, reproducible proof of your gender identity."

"Proof?" Brooke asked. "I always told people I was a woman, but they always had to just take my word for it. You mean I can actually prove it now?"

"The proof is right there," Veronica said. "Empirical evidence. It proves you're a woman. Really, a woman."

"Proof," Brooke said to herself. "Proof," Then she squealed in delight and ran to Geoffrey, coming dangerously close to falling over her heels on the way. "You're keeping this machine here, aren't you?" she asked. "It'll still be here tomorrow?"

"I'm hiring your company to do third-party validation," Geoffrey said. He turned off the machine and then shook her offered hand. "We'll be here as long as it takes."

"Oh, this is so wonderful!" Brooke said. "I can't wait to show everyone. We can call the news. We can show the world!"

"Show the world what?" a feminine voice said from the doorway.

Everyone turned to the source of the voice: a slender woman with short raven-black hair, caucasian skin, ruby lips, and sapphire eyes who was leaning suggestively against the doorframe.

"Justine," Sara said. "Did you see it? We saw Brooke's gender identity. It's pink! She's a woman after all!"

"I saw something," Justine said. She turned to Veronica. "What did I just see?"

Geoffrey stood up straight and began to launch into an explanation, but Justine cut him off.

"She can speak, can't she?" Justine said, nodding toward Veronica.

"Well, of course she can," Geoffrey said.

"Then let's let her," Justine said, returning her full attention to Veronica. "I repeat: What did I just see?"

Veronica eyed Geoffrey nervously. He muttered something under his breath but nodded at her to go ahead. She turned to Justine and answered: "I believe you saw what the rest of us saw: Brooke's gender identity. The pink color proves she's a woman."

Justine looked at the machine, lowering her precisely-plucked eyebrows. "Prove gender identity? That's impossible."

"Not anymore," Geoffrey said, thrusting his chest out. "My invention has turned the impossible into the possible. You saw the results yourself. Proof, real proof, of gender identity."

Justine continued to stare at the machine. "Gender identity doesn't require proof," she said. "Someone tells you what gender they identify as, and you believe them. That's gender identity. Their word is all the proof you need."

"But now we can prove it scientifically!" Geoffrey said. "We're scientists! We don't just accept what someone says. We prove it. That's what science does. And that's what my machine can do. It can prove someone's gender identity!"

Justine turned an icy glare to Geoffrey. "Someone's gender identity is their personal truth," she said. "Their personal truth. It doesn't require proof."

"And now it can become objective truth," Geoffrey said. "Scientific truth." He folded his arms defensively. "Not just personal."

Brooke walked to Justine and laid a large hand on her

arm. "Don't you see, Justine?" Brooke pleaded. "I'm tired of relying on my personal truth. This gives me a chance to objectively prove I am what I say I am. Isn't that wonderful?"

Justine sighed and her icy glare disappeared. "I understand your interest," she told Brooke. Then she addressed Veronica once more: "I assume you've done the necessary preliminary tests already? Both with those who identify as their biological sex and those who identify as a different gender?"

"We've tested over three dozen, I think," Veronica said, looking at Geoffrey for confirmation. "In every case, the machine accurately showed their gender identity."

"So they tell you their gender identity," Justine said, "and then your machine shows you the exact same thing?"

Veronica nodded.

"Here's what I don't understand," Justine said. "With respect, Brooke", she nodded at the other woman and then she continued speaking to Veronica. "Your machine sounds completely unnecessary. All it does is confirm what someone told you themselves. Why not just take their word for it and not insult them by asking them to prove their identity? This is their identity. Why aren't their words good enough?"

"With what other topic would words be good enough?" Geoffrey said. "With what other topic would we not ask for actual, objective, proof rather than just take someone's word for it?"

"Yes, but this is their identity we're talking about," Justine said.

"Yes, and now we can prove their gender identity is a real, literal thing," Geoffrey said. "Without proof, how can you know it isn't just a fantasy?"

Justine turned to Brooke. "You're not insulted by this?"

Brooke shook her head. "Proof would be wonderful," she said.

"And think of the benefits to your company," Geoffrey said. "Millions will jump at the chance to actually prove their identity, and every time someone questions the efficacy of my machine, they will be told how it was extensively tested at Femina Laboratories, putting your company's name out there, free advertising that the entire world will notice."

Justine shook her head. "It's always about money with you men, isn't it? Fine," she said, waving a hand dismissively. "I see your point. Even if I think the machine is completely unnecessary, the world is full of idiots. Many would be interested, and the free publicity would be welcome."

"I can get the test report published for sure," Brooke said. "The publicity is guaranteed."

"I already agreed to it," Justine said. "There's no need to push me anymore." She looked at the machine again. "How does it work anyway?"

As before, she had pointedly addressed this question to Veronica, but Geoffrey answered anyway. "It's this crimson crystal," he said, pointing at the red crystal in the middle of the machine. "When you shine a light through it and you direct that light on someone, their gender identity is visible behind them."

"It behaves like a shadow, I think," Veronica added.

"Okay, but how does it work?" Justine asked impatiently.

"We … we don't know," Veronica said.

"But that doesn't matter," Geoffrey interjected. "There

are lots of things in science we don't fully understand yet. What matters is that it's accurate. 100% accurate! In every case, it has given the correct result. Each and every time it shows a person's gender identity, clear as day."

"Impressive," Justine said, still addressing Veronica. "But if you don't know how the crimson crystal works, how did you know how to make it?"

Veronica looked at Geoffrey.

"You do know how to make it, don't you?" Justine asked.

Neither answered.

Justine laughed. "Are you telling me that's the only crimson crystal you have? What? Did you just find it somewhere?"

Geoffrey sputtered. "It doesn't matter where I found it. It works! 100%! That's what matters!"

Justine raised her hands in exasperation. "Forget what I said earlier. We do science here, not magic shows!"

"But now we can prove I'm a woman!" Brooke said, pleading to Justine. "Don't you understand how important that is to me?"

Justine rolled her eyes. "Fine, fine," she said. Then she raised a finger at Brooke. "This is your project then, and I don't want to hear anything about it. Magic rocks . . . " she scoffed. She looked over at Sara and Sally. "Has she filled out the paperwork yet?"

"Who?" Sara asked. "Brooke?"

"Of course not Brooke," Justine said impatiently. She pointed at Veronica. "This one."

"Umm . . . " Sally said.

Justine rolled her eyes again. "You two," she said to Sally and Sara. "Take them to the front and have them fill out the project paperwork. If we're going to be involved in this farce, I want to make sure we're going to get paid. And you," she said, pointing at Brooke. "Don't you have a train to catch? Do you want to be stuck taking a taxi all the way home again?"

Brooke looked at her watch. "Oh dear!" she said, and she hurried out the door, her stiletto heels clicking down the hall. Justine vanished into the hallway as well.

"We better get your paperwork done," Sara said to Geoffrey.

"It's at the front desk," Sally said.

Geoffrey nodded. "Can we lock the lab when we leave?" he asked.

"The key to the room is back at the front desk," Sara said. "We can get it with the paperwork."

Geoffrey turned to Veronica. "You pack things up here and wait until we get back to lock the door." He followed Sara and Sally toward the hallway, but then stopped and turned back to Veronica. Reaching behind his back, he pulled out a small revolver that had been concealed underneath his shirt. He held it out for Veronica.

"I don't need your gun," Veronica said, grimacing at it. "You'll be less than a minute away."

"Just take it," Geoffrey said. "Just until we secure the room. Don't you realize how much money this invention is worth?"

Veronica smiled at Geoffrey. "We're going to be rich," she said.

Geoffrey offered the gun to her again.

"Put it on the cart if that makes you feel better," Veronica said. She unplugged the power cord from the wall and started rolling it together.

Geoffrey laid his revolver on the cart next to the machine and then followed Sally and Sara back to the front desk, where they handed him a clipboard with the needed paperwork. The blonde twins sat in their receptionist chairs while he stood in front of their desk filling out the paperwork.

Behind the receptionist desk, the wall was filled with pictures of women, each labeled with the designation "Researcher of the Month" and a date.

Geoffrey glanced up at the pictures. "You have a lot of women researchers here," he said.

"We only have women researchers here," Sara said.

"Justine only hires women," Sally said.

"She doesn't like men," Sara said.

Geoffrey paused with his paperwork and peered down at the twins. "Isn't that illegal?"

"No one cares if you discriminate as long as you only discriminate against the right people," Sally said.

"But what about Frantz?" Geoffrey asked. "She hired him didn't she?"

"Oh, Justine doesn't mind hiring men to be janitors or other menial jobs like that," Sara said.

"She thinks all men belong in menial jobs," Sally added. "She says that's why 'menial' starts with 'men'."

Geoffrey set down his pen. "I thought your boss was acting strange back there. Am I making a mistake bringing my business here? Will she even accept business from men?"

"Oh, she accepts business from men as long as they pay her. She wants their money," Sara said.

"She thinks it's poetic justice to use money from men to fund her off-the-books project to create a virus that will eradicate you all," Sally said.

The twins smiled at Geoffrey sweetly.

Geoffrey looked from one twin to the other. "You're

joking, right?"

The twins kept smiling. Sara's right eyebrow twitched. "Yes?" she said.

Geoffrey shook his head. "I'm going to be rich, so who cares." Picking up the pen, he returned to the paperwork.

After a moment of silence, Sara turned to Sally. "This is so awesome," she said.

"I know," Sally said. "And you know what's the most awesome of all?"

"What?" Sara asked.

"We finally get to prove if people really are gender-fluid!" Sally said.

"What do you mean?" Sara asked.

"Well, someone says they're gender-fluid and we all just take their word for it. Doesn't that seem strange to you?" Sally said. "It always seemed strange to me."

Sara nodded in agreement. "Like, imagine if a man showed up and claimed to be from the gas company, and he said he was there to check for a gas leak, but he didn't have a badge or credentials or anything, and we just believed him without asking for proof, and we let him wander around the office by himself."

"We'd get fired for that," Sally said.

"Well, you'd get fired," Sara said, "but I'd have to go home too."

"That's true," Sally said. Then she lowered her voice. "You know what I always wanted to do? Whenever someone claims to be gender-fluid, I always wanted to look them in the eyes and say, 'Prove it!' "

Sara giggled. "You'd get in so much trouble for that!"

Sally giggled as well.

"Well, now you're allowed to ask that question," Geoffrey said. He set the pen down and handed Sally his completed paperwork. "Because now they can answer it with my machine."

Sara's eyes grew wide. "You can prove that someone is gender-fluid?"

Geoffrey smiled at the women. "Their gender identity shows as purple," he said.

"That is so awesome!" Sally said.

"We can prove if people really are gender-fluid!" Sara said.

"Can you show us?" they asked in unison, giant smiles on their faces.

Geoffrey laughed. "I've done tests with three separate people who identify as gender-fluid. I'll see if one or two of them can drop by the lab over the next few days."

"That is so awesome!" Sally said again.

The sharp crack of a gunshot halted their conversation, the bang echoing back and forth in the lobby for what seemed like an eternity. All three of their faces drained of color as they stared at each other and then stared at the open door to the hallway.

There was the sound of running feet and then something heavy struck the floor and a woman yelled, "Help!"

Sara and Sally sprang to their feet, following after Geoffrey, who was already to the hallway doorway. The hallway was deserted, the only light coming from the open door to Lab C and a side corridor further away. Sally and Sara followed after Geoffrey, who sprinted into Lab C.

"No," they heard him yell. "No ... no ... no ..." They hurried through the door and found him kneeling in a circle of red dust.

His crimson crystal had been smashed.

Sally looked behind the machine and gave a startled shout. Geoffrey looked over and sprang to his feet. "No!"

he screamed. He ran to Veronica's body, which lay motionless behind the machine. "No!" He hugged her close. "No!"

"Help me!" a woman yelled again from the hallway. "I got him!" she yelled. "Help me!"

"That's Justine!" Sara said to Sally, who nodded. They both ran out into the hallway, where they heard a commotion coming from the lighted side corridor. Following the noise, they turned to find Justine wrestling with Frantz, who was struggling to get away.

"Call the police!" Justine said. "I got him! Call the police!"

Sara looked at Sally and both of their mouths dropped open.

Detective Sturn held the door for Detective Ortez and then entered the front lobby of Femina Laboratories behind her. A large man with caucasian skin and gray-streaked brown hair, Detective Sturn towered over Detective Ortez, a short woman with light-brown skin and curly brown hair that flowed slightly past her shoulders. Detective Ortez fell in behind Detective Sturn as soon as they had both entered the room. The two detectives studied the room, but Detective Ortez divided her attention between studying the room and studying how Detective Sturn was studying it.

Two pretty blondes sat in chairs behind the receptionist desk. They were resting their chins in their hands, the same shell-shocked look on their faces. In one of the lounge chairs, a middle-aged man sat, his face buried in his hands and his shoulders shaking slightly. A police officer stood discretely nearby. Detective Sturn caught the officer's eye and signaled him over.

"What've we got, Berryfield?" Sturn asked.

"Dead girl in one of the back rooms," Officer Berryfield said. "Single gunshot to the chest."

"And these three?" Sturn said, gesturing at them. "They witnesses?"

"Only to each other's alibis," Berryfield said. "They were all here together in the lobby when it went down."

"Anyone else in the building?"

Berryfield nodded. "Just two: the janitor and the owner. We've swept the rest of the building. Doors are locked. No sign that anyone left."

"So a good chance it was one of them?" Ortez said.

"Looks that way," Berryfield said. He smiled at her. "Long time no see, Karla"

Ortez smiled back. "Three days as a detective and you act like it's been forever." She hugged him.

"Looks like we've got security cameras?" Sturn said, nodding at a small black camera in the corner of the lobby ceiling.

"There's a few sprinkled through the hallways as well. Problem is, they're all fake," Berryfield said.

"Fake?" Ortez asked.

"Yeah, apparently the owner of the place is rather tightfisted with money. That's the way the receptionists put it, in so many words."

"Show us the scene," Sturn said.

Berryfield nodded and led them back into the hallway and then into Lab C. The detectives spread out as they entered the room, both of them noting the details of the scene, although Ortez kept paying equal attention to Sturn and what he was paying attention to.

"Lab goons haven't got here yet," Berryfield said.

"Don't worry, we won't touch anything," Ortez said. She pointed at the revolver lying on the floor. "I assume this is the weapon?"

"Sure seems that way," Berryfield said. "Lab goons will confirm later."

"Gun's owner?" Sturn asked.

"Inventor-dude says it's his," Berryfield said. "He said he left it here for the girl's protection when he went into the lobby with the blonde chicks to fill out the paperwork."

"Inventor-dude?" Ortez said.

Berryfield shrugged. "That's what he is." He pointed at the machine in the middle of the lab. "Whoever shot the girl broke his machine."

They gathered around the young woman's body. Sturn bent to one knee to get a closer look. "Who is she?"

"Veronica Timmer," Berryfield said. "Assistant to inventor-dude ... and lover."

Sturn looked up at Berryfield and raised an eyebrow.

"Tell me about it," Berryfield said. "I'm in the wrong profession."

Ortez snorted. "And about thirty pounds too heavy."

"Hey," Berryfield said. "This isn't fat. It's backup muscle!" He patted his prominent gut.

Sturn stood and looked around the room again.

"Do you think we'll get prints from the gun?" Ortez asked Berryfield.

"I doubt it," Sturn answered. He pointed at a yellow rubber glove that lay discarded against the wall by the doorway.

"I didn't see that," Ortez said. She looked embarrassed by the oversight.

"And any DNA from the glove will be useless," Berryfield said.

"Why?" Sturn asked.

"It's probably from the supply closet. One of the possibles is the janitor. Every glove in the supply closet has his DNA on it. And apparently a lot of gloves in the supply closet have the owner's DNA on them as well. She's a little bit of a neat freak and often redoes jobs herself."

"Says who?" Ortez asked.

"Barbie A and Barbie B," Berryfield replied.

Ortez snorted again.

"Miss me yet, Karla?" Berryfield asked, but Ortez just waved him off.

Sturn was looking from the gun to the glove to the body and back again.

"I know what you're thinking," Berryfield said. "But gunshot residue won't be any good either."

"Why not?" Sturn asked.

"When the first officers arrived at the scene, the janitor and the owner had been going at it for ten minutes. They were tearing into each other worse than two college juniors fighting over who is more woke. If either of them had gunshot residue on them, now both of them do."

"Not helpful," Sturn said.

"It is what it is," Berryfield replied.

Sturn looked back at the machine. "So either the janitor or the owner came into the lab after the three left, shot the woman and broke the machine. Why?"

Berryfield shrugged. "I guess they didn't like the machine."

"What's it do?" Ortez asked.

Berryfield raised his eyebrows. "This is where it gets weird."

Sturn nodded for him to go on.

"Inventor-dude claims his machine could show someone's gender identity. Barbie A and Barbie B corroborated that. They saw two people's gender identity."

"You can't see someone's gender identity," Ortez said. "People just expect you to take their word for it."

"But they did with the machine," Berryfield said. "And inventor-dude claims he has tested it with dozens of people who can verify they have seen their identities as well. He says he has videos back at his office."

"What's this red dust on the ground?" Sturn asked.

"That's how the machine was broken," Berryfield said. "It had a red glass inside, some kind of gem. You shine a light through it and point that light at someone and their gender identity shows up behind them."

"Sounds more like magic than science to me," Ortez said.

"Potayto potahto," Berryfield said.

"You would say that," Ortez said. "You can't even work a smartphone."

Sturn bent over to get a closer look at the red dust on the ground. Then he stood and said to Berryfield, "Let's have a chat with the Barbies."

"I thought you'd never ask," Berryfield said.

Ortez rolled her eyes.

After Sara and Sally had explained everything they had seen, the detectives dove into their opinions about the two suspects.

"Tell us about Frantz," Sturn said.

"He's really nice," Sara said.

"He cleans the floors really well," Sally added helpfully.

"How about his background?" Ortez said. "What can you tell us about that?"

"He's an immigrant from Haiti," Sally said.

"But he's not one of those undocumented immigrants," Sara said, her eyebrow twitching.

"Oh no," Sally added. "Definitely not. He's very documented. We have all his documents." She paused. "... somewhere else."

"And we totally pay him with checks and stuff," Sally continued.

"Definitely, checks," Sara said, with a twitch of her eyebrow. "Lots of checks. Definitely not cash under the table."

"And you keep those check stubs ..." Ortez began.

"Somewhere else," Sally said, smiling up at her.

Ortez snorted in amusement.

"Has he ever been violent before?" Sturn asked.

"Frantz?" Sara said. "Oh no. Nothing like that."

"He has a family," Sally said.

"We've never met them," Sara said.

"But we're sure they're nice," Sally said.

"Do you think Frantz would have a reason to break Geoffrey's machine?" Sturn asked.

"Why would he do that?" Sara asked. "That's just more work for him. Who do you think will be cleaning up all that red dust?"

"And the blood," Sally said.

They both smiled at the detectives sweetly.

"The machine supposedly proved gender identity. Would that upset Frantz?" Sturn asked.

"Why would that upset Frantz?" Sally said. "The machine proved he's a man."

"That's right. We saw it. He's a man. We're witnesses," Sara said.

Sturn glanced at Ortez and then looked back at the twins. "And Justine?"

"She's our boss," Sally said.

"She's your boss," Sara corrected Sally.

"That's right," Sally said. "Sara doesn't work here."

"Whoa, whoa, whoa," Berryfield said. "No one said anything about you not working here. If you don't work here, why are you here?"

Sara shrugged. "I come here because I'm bored. Justine doesn't care as long as she doesn't have to pay me."

"Justine thinks we share the same brain," Sally said.

"She doesn't know we heard her say that," Sara said.

Berryfield looked utterly confused, but Sturn just shrugged. "Has Justine ever been violent?" he asked.

"Justine? No," Sara said.

"Well, not until she was wrestling in the hall with Frantz," Sally said. "That was pretty violent."

"But that's because she thought Frantz was the murderer," Sara said. "So that's pretty normal."

"Do you think Justine could have killed Veronica?" Ortez asked.

"Justine kill a woman?" Sally said. "Justine would never kill a woman."

"Now if it was Geoffrey that had been murdered on the other hand . . . " Sara said.

The twins glanced at each other. Then they turned and smiled at the detectives.

"So, she's a feminist?" Ortez asked.

"Saying that Justine is a feminist is like saying the sun is kind of lukewarm," Sara said.

"That means yes," Sally said. "Really, really, yes."

"Some feminists are not fans of transgenders," Ortez continued.

"That's right," Berryfield said. "I've heard that before. What are they called? Turds or something?"

"They're called Terfs," Sally said. "Trans-exclusionary radical feminists."

Sara smiled at Officer Berryfield. "You're not very good at mansplaining," she said.

"What?" Berryfield asked.

Ortez laughed.

"Justine isn't a Terf," Sally said.

"How do you know?" Sturn asked.

The twins swiveled their chairs in unison to face the wall behind them. Sara pointed at a picture of Brooke.

"See this woman?" Sally asked.

The detectives and Officer Berryfield all leaned closer to look at the picture of Brooke. "Researcher of the Month, March 2019," was written in the plaque below.

"That's no woman," Berryfield said.

The twins spun their chairs around to face him. "Yes, she is," Sara said.

"We saw her gender identity." Sally said. "Her body is male, but her gender identity is female. The machine proved it."

"The machine which was broken," Ortez said. "Is there a reason why Justine wouldn't want Brooke to have proof she is a woman? Some sort of compensation issue?"

Sturn shook his head. "I don't see how. Maybe something personal against Brooke?"

"Count the pictures," Sara said to the detectives.

"What?" Ortez asked.

"Count the number of times Justine picked Brooke as researcher of the month," Sally said.

The detectives studied the pictures. There were a few dozen, all women, with at least a dozen different women appearing at least once, and Brooke's picture was there at least a third of the time.

"Justine loves Brooke," Sara said.

"Why?" Sturn asked.

"Because Brooke is a good researcher," Sally said.

"And because she cut off her male parts," Sara said.

Sally nodded. "Mainly because she cut off her male parts."

"What?" Berryfield exclaimed, his eyes wide.

"Justine doesn't like men," Sara said. "And Brooke didn't want to be a man so bad she cut off her male parts."

"Snip, snip!" Sally said.

The twins smiled innocently.

Berryfield's face turned green and he hurried outside.

"Thanks for your time," Sturn said to the twins.

"Can we go home now?" Sara asked. "The Bachelorette is on."

"Not yet," Sturn said. "We might have more questions."

Geoffrey wasn't any more helpful than the twins had been.

"What do you mean you just found the crimson crystal? Where did you find it? At a garage sale?" Ortez asked in exasperation.

Geoffrey avoided her gaze. "You wouldn't believe me."

"Try us," Sturn said.

Geoffrey was silent for a moment. Then he gave himself a brief nod and started talking. "There was a bright light and then a loud boom. I thought ... I don't know what I thought ... but I went outside to investigate and that's when I found it. A meteorite had fallen into my yard. I'm not sure how big it had been originally because I don't know what it was made of, but it left a three-feet-wide crater on impact."

"How do you not know what it was made of? Didn't you have it tested?" Ortez asked.

"It disintegrated," Geoffrey said. "I touched it gently with a stick and it just fell apart and blew away. The only thing left was the crimson crystal."

"A gem just fell out of the sky that let you see people's gender identity?" Ortez said.

"You don't understand," Geoffrey said. "I could have made millions, millions! But now it's gone. There was only one crimson crystal like that. Now it's gone, gone!"

"And Veronica is dead," Sturn said.

"Veronica," Geoffrey said softly. He buried his face in his hands and refused to answer any more questions.

Berryfield returned a few minutes later, looking less green. He prepped the detectives on their talk with the two suspects. Standing in front of Justine's closed office door, Berryfield said, "This one is something else."

"Can't handle a woman?" Ortez said. "You're getting soft."

Berryfield shook his head. "You don't know what you're talking about," he said. "We don't have any female officers on patrol around here tonight. Everyone that reported to the scene was a man, and I kid you not, every second sentence out of this one was some complaint about our 'male gaze' or our 'male privilege'. You have no idea how long she droned on about the patriarchy and how horrible it is." Berryfield turned to Sturn. "Did you know you're part of the patriarchy, Sturn?" Berryfield asked. "Apparently all men are. Somehow, someone forgot to send my membership card in the mail. Anyway, you'd think that when someone was murdered in her building that she'd be a little more cooperative, but apparently that's asking for too much from Ms Ice Queen."

"You're just full of nicknames tonight," Ortez said.

"It's what I do," Berryfield said. "But just wait. You'll

see."

Sturn glanced at Ortez. "I guess you'll be doing the talking," he said.

Ortez grunted. "Sure, give me the easy one."

Justine sat behind a large carved wooden desk. She leaned back in a tall leather chair that likely would have cost the detectives a week's salary. She was pressing an ice pack against her forehead, and her shirt was wrinkled, its top buttons broken off and exposing a considerable amount of cleavage, but all things considered she looked remarkably good for someone who had been wrestling so intensely shortly before.

She was a dangerously attractive woman, and Detective Sturn felt immediately drawn to her on a primal level, but he was no fool. She was incredibly alluring yes: her athletic build, her makeup composed just so, seemingly undisturbed by the wrestling match; but her allure was the allure of a praying mantis. She was the kind of woman who didn't doll herself up to attract men, she dolled herself up to taunt them. Any man who fell for her lures would likely end up the same way as the male praying mantis: missing his head.

"It's simple really," Justine said after Ortez asked her to tell what happened. "I was in my office, preparing to head home for the day, when I heard the gunshot. Now, I know what I should have done: I should have hidden under my desk and called the police. I don't know what I was thinking, but this is my lab. Someone was shooting a gun in my lab. And I guess part of me just wasn't going to let that happen, and before I knew it, I was out in the hallway, and that's when I saw him."

"Frantz?" Ortez asked.

"He burst out of the lab, and right then we met eyes,

and I saw something wild there, something mad. I've never seen that before," Justine said. "Not in him. Not in anyone else."

"Why did you chase him?" Ortez asked.

"Well I couldn't just let him get away, could I?" Justine said. "He shot someone in my lab. In my lab!"

"How did you know he shot someone?" Ortez asked.

"You didn't see the look in his eyes," Justine said. "It was like he was a wild beast at the moment, and I just knew, I just knew. And I knew I couldn't let him get away with it."

"So you tackled him and held him until the police arrived?"

"That's right."

"Why would Frantz do something like this?"

Justine was quiet for a moment. "I've been thinking it over since it happened," she said. Then she lowered her voice. "You know he's from Haiti."

"Yes ... " Ortez said slowly.

"They are such violent people, the Haitians," Justine said. "The crime in their country, you know, it's horrible."

"So, he's a violent person because he's a Haitian?" Ortez said. Her voice had taken on a dangerous tone. Sturn grunted a warning at her.

"Oh, I'm not saying anything racial," Justine said. "I'm talking culturally. He was raised with violence like it was mother's milk. How could I not have expected him to snap in that way? I really should have seen it coming. I almost feel guilty about it."

"But then how could you have hired a janitor on subsistence wages and paid him under the table?" Ortez said. Sturn grunted another warning.

Justine's eyes narrowed. "Who told you that?" she

asked.

"We could check your books if you like," Ortez said.

Justine was quiet for a moment. "I have disagreements with our immigration laws," she said. "And at times I choose to act in civil disobedience to those laws. People are not illegal," she said. "It's wrong for our country to treat them that way. As a privileged individual, it's my responsibility to help the marginalized, so I try to help where I can, but sometimes my judgment is faulty and I help the wrong person, as in this case."

"So you did it out of the goodness of your heart?" Ortez said. She was about to say something else but Sturn, tired of his grunts being ignored, put a heavy hand on her shoulder. Ortez flinched slightly under the weight. She took a deep breath and continued in a more level voice. "So you claim his background makes him prone to violence," she said, "but why would he attack Veronica? What is his motive? And why would he want to destroy the machine? Why wouldn't he want people to be able to prove their gender identity was real?"

"I've thought about that as well," Justine said. "He's Catholic, you know. Have you seen that gaudy crucifix he wears around his neck? Now, I'm not positive about this—it's just a theory—but as I've been sitting here trying to think why he would do it, a question occurred to me: What would the Pope think if a Catholic let gender identity be proven? That would practically prove Catholicism was wrong!"

Ortez raised an eyebrow skeptically. "I don't know about that."

Justine continued: "And, I don't know if I should mention this or not, but last Pride Month he was the only employee who didn't wear a rainbow ribbon to work."

"You require your employees to wear rainbow ribbons?" Ortez asked.

"We don't explicitly require them to, no," Justine said. "But why wouldn't he choose to? What does that say about him?"

"And how about you?" Ortez asked. "What do you think about gender identity?"

Justine raised her eyebrows, "I don't understand what you mean," she said. "That's like asking what I think about photosynthesis. Gender identity simply is. What am I supposed to think about it?"

"What do you think about Geoffrey's machine?" Ortez asked. "What do you think about being able to prove that gender identity is real?"

Justine waved her hand. "Oh, that. I thought the whole idea was silly. Gender identity is how you identify yourself. Proof isn't necessary. People declare what gender they identify as, and then we affirm their identity. I see no reason why some machine should be brought into the picture. It seems completely superfluous to me."

"So you have no problem with gender identity?" Ortez asked.

"Absolutely not. That's like having a problem with thermodynamics. It simply is."

"And you have no problem with proving someone's gender identity?"

Justine shrugged. "It's always interesting to prove things, but frankly I find the whole idea a little insulting, don't you? It's like carding a seventy-year-old woman when she wants to buy wine. You already know the answer because they already told you the answer, and that should be good enough. Why insult them by demanding proof? It's their identity we're talking about. You got all the proof you needed when they told you what gender they identified as."

"But someone might not believe them," Ortez said. "Someone might want proof."

"I suppose that's true. Some people can be so cynical and untrusting, that's unfortunately true. And there's always the financial angle too, although I'm almost ashamed to admit it. Being the lab that tested the machine would have been very lucrative. It's a pity that Frantz destroyed it. There was only one crimson crystal, you know. Without that, the machine doesn't work."

"What a pity," Ortez said.

Finished with Ms Ice Queen, the detectives turned their attention to the other suspect. Frantz had been placed into a large supply closet, which had been emptied of supplies. After the detectives entered the large closet, they asked the officer standing guard to step outside. Then they watched as Frantz paced back and forth on the other side of the closet, rubbing his crucifix while he muttered something to himself. He didn't seem to have noticed they were there.

"What's he saying?" Sturn asked Ortez.

"He's speaking in French, not Spanish," Ortez said.

"But can't you get the gist of it?" Sturn asked.

Ortez sighed and concentrated on Frantz's words.

"I think he's saying the Lord's Prayer," she said.

Sturn nodded. Then he spoke loudly, "Frantz, we'd like to speak with you."

Frantz froze, raising wild eyes to look at them. Suddenly he darted for the door, as if he could get past a man twice his size. Detective Sturn raised his left hand and grabbed the smaller man, holding him gently. "Let's just have a chat," he said.

"I can't go," Frantz said, struggling against Sturn's

grip. "I can't go."

"You can't go where?" Ortez asked.

"I have a family!" Frantz said. "I can't go!"

Ortez nodded in understanding. "We're not immigration, Frantz."

Frantz paused in his struggling and looked at the two of them, but apparently he didn't like what he saw because he muttered something under his breath and tried to wiggle out of Detective Sturn's grip again. Sturn pushed him gently back to the other side of the large closet.

"I can't go! I can't go!" Frantz wailed.

"Listen, if you did nothing wrong, there's no reason for immigration to be involved, do you understand me?" Ortez said. "Isn't that right, Detective Sturn?"

Sturn shrugged. Then he nodded. "Why would we need immigration? We're just chatting here."

"Why don't you tell us what happened?" Ortez said.

Frantz looked from one detective to the other, visibly shaking, but he didn't try to make a run for it again. Holding his crucifix for support, Franz answered in a thick accent: "I was mopping when I heard the gun. I wanted to run, but my legs wouldn't move. When they started moving, the boss tackled me. She wouldn't let me go. Then I got put in here."

Sturn leaned forward. "Did you shoot Veronica?"

Frantz's eyes grew wide. "Who is Veronica?"

"The redheaded woman," Sturn said.

"No, no, no. Why would I shoot anyone?" Frantz said.

"How about the machine?" Ortez asked.

"Which machine?"

"The machine in Lab C," Sturn said.

Frantz nodded in recognition. "It showed my soul," he said.

"Right, it showed your gender identity," Ortez said.

Frantz nodded again. "I have a man's soul," he said with satisfaction in his voice.

"That's right," Ortez said. "Does it bother you when someone has a different gender identity than their body? Would it have bothered you if the machine showed that you, a man, had a female gender identity?"

Frantz frowned. "Why would the machine show me with a woman's soul? I have a man's soul."

Ortez looked at Sturn and gave a slight shrug.

"Did you want to destroy the machine?" Sturn asked.

"Why would I want to destroy the machine?" Frantz said. "It showed my soul!"

After speaking with Frantz, the detectives huddled in the hallway with Officer Berryfield. "So what's the plan, boss?" Berryfield said to Detective Sturn. "We're already pushing it as it is. Anything else and we really should be bringing them in, otherwise we've got to let them go."

The three paused as Veronica's body was wheeled out of the lab and then down the hall to the backdoor, avoiding the lobby where Geoffrey still grieved.

Sturn turned to Ortez. "What do you think?"

Ortez shrugged. "Justine is a piece of work, but I don't see a motive there. The problem is I don't see a motive for Frantz either."

"He sure does seem excited about something though," Berryfield said.

"For good reason," Ortez said. "How would you like to be deported even though you did nothing wrong?"

"If he came here illegally then he came here illegally," Berryfield said. "That's something wrong."

Sturn held up a large hand to stop the argument.

"How about you," Ortez said to Sturn. "Do you have

any ideas?"

"Just one," Sturn said. "A bit crazy," he said, "but it's been a crazy night." He leaned toward Ortez and whispered something in her ear. Her eyes brightened and she gave a small smile. "Do you really think?" she asked.

"We'll see," Sturn said. Then he turned to Berryfield. "Tell Justine she can go home, but ask her to come by Lab C first. We have one last question."

Detective Sturn was facing the far wall of Lab C when Justine entered the room. She scowled when she saw Detective Ortez wasn't there, but apparently the prospect of going home was sufficiently enticing that she deemed to address a male.

"I was told you had a final question before I could go home?" Justine said.

Sturn waved her over. "Come over here and take a look at this."

Justine hesitated for a moment, glancing at the red dust and blood that still lay on the floor, but then she walked over beside him and looked at the wall. "What am I supposed to be looking at?"

Just then, Detective Ortez entered the room with Geoffrey.

"Did you get it from him?" Sturn asked Ortez.

Ortez raised her hand quickly, something red in her hand flashing briefly before she closed it again.

Justine stood up straight. "What is that?" she asked.

"It's the backup crimson crystal," Sturn said. "Geoffrey kept it in his car. It turns out the machine isn't broken after all."

Geoffrey looked up sharply at Sturn, but thankfully he remained quiet.

"I don't understand," Justine said.

"Go ahead and install it," Sturn said to Ortez.

She walked to the machine and then turned her back to Sturn and Justine as she fiddled with its insides. Then she dragged the cord to the wall and plugged it in before turning back to Detective Sturn and nodding her head.

"You can turn it on now, Geoffrey," Sturn said.

"What's going on?" Justine said, her hands now clenched into fists. "You said there was only one crimson crystal!" she said to Geoffrey.

Geoffrey looked from the machine to Detective Sturn and back again.

Sturn stepped away from Justine, leaving her standing alone in front of the machine.

"You told me there was only one crimson crystal!" she said again. "There wasn't supposed to be a backup one! You weren't supposed to know how to make more!"

Geoffrey looked at Justine. Then he looked at Detective Sturn. Detective Sturn nodded. Geoffrey's eyes narrowed and he walked toward the machine.

"What are you doing?" Justine said. She was shaking now. "The machine was supposed to be broken!"

Geoffrey reached the machine. He raised his hand to flip the switch.

"STOP!" Justine screamed, and Geoffrey froze. The whole room stared at her.

"Just stop," she whispered, looking down at the ground, her raven-black hair falling in front of her face.

Sturn winked at Ortez and she smiled. "What's wrong, Justine?" Ortez asked. "Why shouldn't we turn on the machine? What are you afraid to see? What are you afraid we'll see?"

Justine spoke so softly it was almost as if she were speaking to only herself. "It's my gender identity," she said. "My gender identity. I get to choose it. You don't get to force one on me. It's my choice. It's my gender identity."

"And everyone should just take your word for it?" Ortez asked.

"Of course they should. Who could be a better judge of my gender identity than myself?" Justine said. "It's my gender identity."

"That's fine if gender identity is just a wish or a fantasy," Ortez said. "If that's all gender identity is, then it's fine to just take your word for it. But if gender identity is something that actually exists in the real world, then why should we assume your judgment is accurate? Sometimes people are wrong."

"And sometimes people lie," Sturn said.

"I am a woman," Justine said.

"Biologically, yes," Sturn said. "But what about your gender identity?"

"My gender identity is female!" Justine said. "I choose my gender identity! It's up to me!"

"Do you choose your height?" Sturn asked. "Do you choose your age? No. They are part of reality."

Ortez followed Sturn's lead. "And some people aren't happy with their height or their age, are they?" she said. "Some want to be taller, some want to be shorter, some want to be older, some want to be younger—some want reality to be different than it is. If gender identity isn't just a wish or a fantasy, if it isn't just a deep desire of your heart, if gender identity actually is part of reality, then why should we expect anything different?"

"And proof makes it reality," Sturn said.

Ortez nodded in agreement. "If we just take your word for it, then it's nothing but a fantasy," she said, "but if there is real, actual proof, then gender identity ceases to be a fantasy and it becomes reality instead. Now, with proof, your gender identity isn't female just because you tell us it's female. Now your gender identity is female only if you can prove it's female. And that's not what the machine is going to show us, is it, Justine?"

"I'm a woman!" Justine wailed, dropping to her knees. "Look at me!" She tore at her shirt, popping more buttons and exposing a utilitarian bra. "Test my blood! I'm a woman!"

"But your biological sex was never the issue, your gender identity was," Ortez said. "And you don't get to claim your gender identity is female and expect us to just take your word for it anymore, not now that there's proof. It's science now, not fantasy. Your gender identity isn't what you claim it to be anymore. It isn't what you choose it to be. Your gender identity is whatever the proof proves it to be. And what will Geoffrey's machine prove your gender identity to be? What have you always known proof, actual scientific proof, would prove your gender identity to be?"

"But the machine is broken! It's not supposed to work anymore!" Justine pointed at Geoffrey. "You lied to me! There wasn't supposed to be another crimson crystal! Breaking the one was supposed to have been enough. Otherwise I wouldn't have ... "

"Wouldn't have what?" Sturn asked. "Wouldn't have killed Veronica?"

"I didn't want to," Justine whispered, raven-black hair falling again over her downcast eyes. "But she wouldn't let me—"

"Murderer!" Geoffrey yelled. He started toward her, rage in his eyes, but Detective Sturn raised a large hand signaling him to stop and that simple act of resistance was all it took. Geoffrey crumbled to the floor in a ball, weeping. Detective Sturn had Officer Berryfield escort Geoffrey out of the room.

"This isn't how it's supposed to be," Justine said, looking down at the ground. "Gender identity isn't supposed to be real. It's supposed to be a fantasy. It's supposed to be my fantasy. It isn't supposed to be something that can be proven to be different than what I want it to be."

"But Geoffrey's machine changed all that," Ortez said. "It provided proof. It changed gender identity from fantasy to reality."

Justine sat in silence.

"And reality isn't always fair," Sturn said. "It isn't always what we want it to be. So if gender identity is reality . . . "

". . . then some of us will be genders we don't want to be," Ortez finished.

"I'm not a man," Justine wailed. "I'm not! I'm a woman!"

Ortez glanced at Sturn, who nodded. "I have good news, Justine," Ortez said. "You're right. You are a woman. Geoffrey's machine was destroyed, so gender identity is just the fantasy it always was. The only proof that exists, the only actual evidence, is your physical body. You are a woman and no one can prove otherwise—you saw to that. Was it worth it?"

Detective Sturn signaled to Officer Berryfield, who took out his handcuffs.

"I don't understand," Justine said. "What about the backup crimson crystal?

"Oh, you mean this?" Ortez asked. She held up the red object she had briefly flashed in her hand before: the red cover of a brake light. "Just because someone tells you something, doesn't mean it's actually true. You shouldn't have taken our word for it."

Justine gave a soft laugh. "Tricky girl," she said.

Officer Berryfield lifted Justine to her feet. He pulled her hands behind her back and cuffed them.

Justine lifted her head proudly, shaking her hair out of her face as she addressed Detective Ortez one last time. "At least it was a woman that outsmarted me."

"Oh this?" Ortez said, holding up the brake light cover. She pointed at Sturn. "That was his idea."

Justine howled and howled.

Sally and Sara watched as Officer Berryfield dragged a cursing Justine out of the building.

"This sucks," Sara said.

"It totally sucks," Sally agreed. "Now we'll never have proof if people really are gender-fluid or not."

Sara sighed. "I guess we'll just have to take their word for it."

It's Gender-Obscuring, Not Gender-Affirming

The phrase "gender-affirming care" is religious terminology. The "gender" this phrase refers to is the unmeasurable, unfalsifiable concept of gender identity, wherein someone tells you they are male, or female, or non-binary, or two-spirit, or gender-fluid, or whatever the latest fad is, and you're supposed to simply believe them. They could be wrong. They could be lying. You don't know! But that's okay because you have faith, and if someone self-identifies as a particular gender, then they must be right ... right?

I, for one, lack the faith required to believe that.

Every society will have a shared reality. It is inevitable. Without one, a society couldn't function as a society. For most of human history, this shared reality has been dictated by those in power, but secularism proposed something different. Instead of having our shared reality be dictated to us by whoever held the most power, secularism said it should be based on proof, thereby protecting us from religious domination and granting us individual religious freedom. In a secular society, provable reality is our shared reality

There is much more I want to say on this topic, but

I will add just one additional point for now: provable reality is not the same thing as ultimate truth. Consider the existence of God. I believe God exists, but I cannot prove it to you, therefore the existence of God is not part of provable reality, which means that, according to the agreement of secularism, I cannot force you to accept that belief as part of our shared reality. So why should we support this agreement if it means the shared reality of society won't be based entirely on what we ourselves consider to ultimately be true? We should support it because this agreement applies to everyone: to me, to you, and to everyone else. And it is through this agreement that we all receive protection from religious domination (from each other) and are guaranteed individual religious freedom. We all agree that provable reality will serve as the foundation necessary for our society to function, and as for everything that is outside the realm of proof (the meaning of life, etc), we agree to disagree.

I wish that more religious people would understand this: In the conflict with the LGBT movement, secularism is our friend, not our foe. Secularism declares that our shared reality must be based solely on proof, *but gender identity is an unprovable belief.* In other words, by forcing their belief in gender identity on others, the LGBT movement is violating secularism. On this topic, secularism is on the side of religious conservatives. If this seems like a hard idea to accept given the current direction of society, then let me point out that the implementation of secularism in the USA today is flawed. We are protected from religious domination by organized religions, but we are not currently protected from religious domination by faith-based movements that claim to not be religious. This is a serious flaw. We need to fix it.

But let me return to the phrase "gender-affirming care". This "gender" LGBT fundamentalists are referring to is outside the realm of proof. We know this because they rely on self-identity to determine someone's "gender" instead of empirical tests. You aren't a "two-spirit" because you took a blood test and it came back "two-spirit". You're a "two-spirit" because you said you were a "two-spirit". That's not secularism. In secularism, when we want to know how tall someone is, we measure them. When we want to know how much someone weighs, we weigh them. When we want to know someone's biological sex, we test their anatomy/DNA. That is what secularism is: a shared reality based solely on proof.

So what is gender according to provable reality? It's our biological sex—because that's what is actually provable. The word "gender" is simply a euphemism for the word "sex". And so, the phrase "gender-affirming care" is nonsense in a secular context. This phrase is talking about cutting off the breasts of teenage girls, about castrating boys, about constructing imitation genitals. That isn't gender-affirming. It's gender-obscuring.

To obscure is to hide or to conceal, and that is exactly what these medical procedures are meant to do. They are trying to conceal a person's provable gender (their biological sex). They are trying to make a person's gender appear to be the opposite of what it actually is.

You are free to believe in gender identity, just like I am free to believe in God, but I can't force you to accept my unprovable belief in God, and you can't force me to accept your unprovable belief in gender identity. "Gender-affirming" is religious terminology. In a secular society, these medical procedures are gender-obscuring.

A Principal's Conundrum

"Thank you for meeting with me," Mr. Smith said.

"Of course," Principal Olsen said, settling back in his chair. "My secretary mentioned you had some concerns following our recent assembly about gender identity?"

"Yes, I was wondering if you could give me a list of the gender identities that students are expected to believe in?"

"A list?" Principal Olsen asked. "That's not really the way it works. What we are trying to impress on our students is how important gender identity is and how they must affirm the gender identities of their fellow classmates. The central message we are teaching them is that everyone's gender identity is an innate part of themselves, so to answer your question about what identities they need to believe in: All of them."

Mr. Smith sat back in his chair, and arched his fingers. "So, just to take a random gender identity as an example, you expect all your students to believe in two-spirits?"

"Of course."

Mr. Smith raised an eyebrow, the corners of his mouth rising into a slight smile. "Do you even know what the two-spirit gender identity is?"

Principal Olsen rocked back on his chair. "Well … I … well … that is … it's hard to keep track of all of them … "

"Yes, and new ones keep getting invented every week," Mr. Smith agreed.

"Well, yes, but um, about two-spirit. I believe it is something related to Native American culture."

"Yes, it's kind of a hodgepodge since it's an umbrella term invented by modern activists to describe what they claim are spiritual traditions from multiple Native American cultures," Mr. Smith said. "But I think it can be described as a person who has two spirits, a male spirit and a female spirit. It's right there in the name."

"Ah yes," Principal Olsen said. "That does ring a bell. I believe you're right. It's right there in the name after all!"

"So if a student identifies as a two-spirit, you expect all the other students to believe them? Just like if a boy identifies as a girl, then you expect the other students to believe he actually *is* a girl?"

"Because then *she* actually would be a girl, yes. Who would know better what gender a person is than themselves? So, yes, of course we expect our students to believe each other's gender identity."

"Including if a student identifies as two-spirit?"

"Definitely."

"Whoa!" Mr. Smith yelled, throwing up his arms. "Do you mean to tell me that you, the principal of a public school, require your students to believe in the existence of the human soul? In a public school!"

Principal Olsen's eyes widened, his chair squeaking as he leaned forward in surprise. "No, no, that's not it at all," he said. "Of course we don't require students to believe in the soul or any religious belief like that."

"But that's what a spirit is, a soul, and how can someone have two souls if souls don't exist? And you just told me yourself that you expect all your students to believe each other's gender identities, including two-spirits."

"Well, yes," Principal Olsen scrambled, "but there are other ways of looking at this. A spirit could be more of a metaphorical thing, so it's more that we're respecting their right to believe what they believe and to express it in the words they choose to use."

"So basically you tell your students: 'You have to believe that student is a two-spirit', but when you say 'two-spirit' you make air quotes?"

"Well, I mean, we can't really require that students believe in someone else's religious beliefs, so, yes, I guess the expectation here would be more of a respect of their beliefs than an actual demand that you believe them yourself."

"Whoa! Whoa!" Mr. Smith yelled, throwing up his arms again. "My daughter identifies as a two-spirit! Do you mean to say that you're going to tell students they don't have to actually believe in her gender identity? You're going to allow students to discriminate against her gender identity just because it isn't a boring vanilla boy or girl one? Air quotes for 'two-spirit'? I can't believe you said that!"

"What?" Principal Olsen said, his face growing pale as he ran his hands wildly through his hair. "Your daughter, a two-spirit? But I thought that was only for Native Americans ..."

Mr. Smith scowled. "Who are you to decide who gets to identify as what gender identity? You said so yourself: It's innate. If it's innate, then it's innate, and who gives you the right to police what is innate to someone else? Are you suggesting that someone could be wrong about their gender identity? Don't you know the APA claims that attempting to change someone's gender identity is harmful to them? Besides, why are you assuming we're not Native American?"

Principal Olsen stammered, "But your last name is Smith!"

"So a Native American can't be named Smith?"

"I guess that would be possible," Principal Olsen said. Then he gingerly asked, "Are you?"

"My daughter identifies as two-spirit," Mr. Smith said, holding up one finger. "And gender identity is innate and no one knows someone's gender better than themselves," he said, holding up a second finger. "And, according to you, only Native Americans can identify as two-spirit." He held up a third finger. "Does that answer your question?"

"I ... I guess it does," Principal Olsen said. "I guess if your daughter identifies as a two-spirit, then she must be Native American."

"Exactly, and it sounds like you're planning to let your students discriminate against her gender identity. You said so yourself! I bet you wouldn't treat a trendy gender identity that way," Mr. Smith said. Then he wiggled all his fingers in the air and spoke in a little girl's voice, "Oh, look at me, I'm non-binary!" Then, dropping his hands to the arms of his chair, he said in a normal voice, "You wouldn't discriminate against my daughter if she said that, I bet!"

Principal Olsen shook his head. "You're absolutely right," he said. "I apologize completely. I'm just ... a little confused at all the .... all the jumping around this conversation is taking. But I promise you as long as I am the principal of this elementary school that no one will discriminate against your daughter's gender identity as a two-spirit!"

"So you promise me you're going to walk down the hallway to each student, and you're going to look them in the eyes, and you're going to shake your finger at them authoritatively, and you're going to tell them, 'This is Mr. Smith's daughter, and she is a two-spirit, and you're required to believe it!' "

"Absolutely," Principal Olsen said. "In fact, I can promise you I will do that tomorrow morning first thing!"

"Whoa! Whoa! Whoa!" Mr. Smith yelled, throwing his arms in the air for the third time. "My son is an atheist! Are you telling me you're going to demand that my atheist son believes in the existence of the human soul? Here, in a public school?"

Principal Olsen blinked, his face now completely drained of color. "Wait ... what?"

"This is a public school," Mr. Smith said, shaking his head in disgust. "Have you ever heard of the US Constitution? Have you ever heard of the Establishment Clause? You can't go around preaching religion in public school! You can't go around demanding that students believe in Native American religious traditions!"

"But I thought you were Native American?"

"If I were Irish, would that mean I'd want you to preach Catholicism to my atheist son?"

"What? I don't ... "

"So let me get this straight," Mr. Smith said, leaning forward in his chair. "I send my son and my daughter to your public school, trusting you to do your civic duty, trusting you to affirm my daughter's gender identity, trusting you to respect my son's atheism, and you're telling me that you're either going to discriminate against my daughter's two-spirit gender identity or else you're going to preach Native American religious traditions to my atheist son? What kind of a school are you running here anyway?"

"I . . . " Principal Olsen said, his eyes blinking rapidly as he started to sway. "I . . . " Then he passed out, his head crashing on the desk with a thud.

Mr. Smith chuckled and rolled his eyes. "Progressives."

‘What Is a Woman?’ Answered

How should we as a society decide what is and what isn’t part of our shared reality? Because every society has a shared reality. It is inevitable. Consider something as mundane as traffic laws. In some nations, people drive on the right. In other nations, people drive on the left. Right or left doesn’t really make much difference, but what makes a difference is this: Everyone has to agree what is right and what is left! We can’t have people deciding “their truth” is that right is left or left is right. That would make our traffic laws useless. We all have to have one shared understanding, one shared reality, upon which our laws and policies can be based.

It is the same for all concepts, including the words “man” and “woman”. If we as a society are going to have laws and policies based on these concepts, then we need to have a common understanding of what these concepts actually are. No “my truth” or “your truth”, we need a shared reality.

But today, when it comes to “man” and “woman”, we clearly don’t agree on how to define the words. Two opposing definitions are in common use, one proof-based and one faith-based.

The Proof-Based Definition

The proof-based definition of "woman" is simple: A woman is an adult human female.

This definition is proof-based because it is based on a person's biological sex, which can be determined through empirical evidence: anatomy and DNA. And because it is proof-based, we are able to know if someone *actually is* a woman or not, no faith required.

(As an aside, lawmakers in some states have made the horrible mistake of allowing legal "sex changes" even though it is biologically impossible to actually change your sex today. This creates the absurd situation where a person could be a biological male yet a legal female, which turns the terms "male" and "female" into legal fiction. These laws are a horrible mistake and a violation of secularism. They should be repealed where present and blocked from being enacted everywhere else. But because of their presence, note that when I say "female", I obviously mean "biological female".)

The Faith-Based Definition

Believers in the LGBT faith-based movement are curiously unable to provide a coherent definition of the word "woman". On their first attempt, they typically use a circular definition where they define the word "woman" using the word "woman". They know what it means in their head, but they can't seem to figure out a way to express it in words. So allow me to do so on their behalf.

Here is the faith-based definition of "woman": A woman is an adult human who self-identifies as a female.

This definition is faith-based because it is based on self-identity, which you have no way to prove or disprove. How do you know they aren't wrong? How do you know they aren't joking? How do you know they aren't lying? You don't. If you believe, you believe based on faith. With the faith-based definition of "woman", it's impossible for you to actually *know* if someone is a woman or not. (They could, for example, change their reported self-identity tomorrow.)

Notice that both definitions start with the proof-based concept of a female, which is all the proof-based definition needs: "The empirical evidence proves this person is a female? Then she's a woman. Case closed."

But the faith-based definition isn't satisfied with this dependence on proof: "Proof this. Proof that. What about My Truth! What about gender identity!"

Sure, gender identity is an unmeasurable, unverifiable, unfalsifiable belief that therefore cannot be proven to even exist, but people *believe* it exists, so they insert a proof-bypass into the definition of "woman", removing any requirement to actually *prove* someone is a female and simply allowing them to *self-identify* as one instead.

There Is No Dictionary God

People often hide behind definitions. "Don't look at me. That's just how the word is defined. I didn't make the rules!" But there is no Dictionary God who will strike you down with a lightning bolt if you don't use the "right" definition, and in this case, what is the "right" definition anyway? Hundreds of millions of people use the proof-based definition of "woman". Are they wrong? Says who? There is no Dictionary God.

And so, in situations like this, where there are two competing definitions for a word in common usage, which definition we choose to use reveals a lot about ourselves. Because why else would you choose to insert a proof-bypass into the definition of "woman" unless you really believed there was an invisible concept of gender identity, something so core to the meaning of life that it should override empirical reality itself. And can you prove that? Absolutely not. The meaning of life is unprovable. Self-identity is unprovable. You are operating entirely on faith, and you are seeking to impose your faith-based beliefs onto a secular society, and that reveals a lot about you.

What Is the Secular Definition?

Now let's return to the topic of reality. There are two competing definitions of "woman" in our society, so which definition should be used as part of our shared reality? I think this all comes down to a simple question: Do we want to live in a secular society, or do we want to live in a society that is dominated by a faith-based movement?

Because if we choose to continue to be a secular society, then that means our shared reality must be based on proof, and so the secular definition of "woman" is obvious. It is the provable one: A woman is an adult human female. In other words, in our shared reality, gender is simply a euphemism for the word "sex", not a separate unprovable concept that overrides biological sex.

People can believe whatever faith-based beliefs they choose. I, myself, am an openly religious man and believe many things based on faith instead of empirical proof, but when it comes to the shared reality of our society, when it comes to that which our laws and policies are based on, we all must defer to what is provable. If we don't, then we turn secularism into a lie.

Secularism or Faith-Based Tyranny

Why does any of this matter? It matters because there are people in our society today who self-identify as transgenders, and we need to know if the word "transgender" means "someone who *believes* their gender is different than their sex", or if it means "someone whose gender *actually is* different than their sex".

The proof, and its lack, is clear. The question is whether you will abide by the truce of secularism and defer to that proof, or will you follow the path of the tyrant and fight to impose your faith-based beliefs onto unbelievers like me.

The Psychologist

Miss Clarke, a petite woman in a dark sweater and jeans who looked barely older than the high school students she taught, stormed into Principal Allen's office. The office was a perfect square, with a single window behind Principal Allen's desk, two chairs positioned in front of it, and a handful around the walls on both sides. Principal Allen was already seated behind his desk, a man and woman in their forties sitting in the chairs facing him. Miss Clarke strode to a chair along the wall and sat perched on the edge, her hands clasped, her eyes blazing.

Principal Allen's eyes narrowed as he looked at her. "Thank you for joining us, Miss Clarke."

She gave a jerky nod. "Is this them?"

"Yes," he said. "But I've just been told there's more to the story than you shared with me earlier."

"The little prick pissed on my desk in front of the entire class! What more to the story could there be?"

The man and woman in the center of the room stiffened. "Now wait just one minute," the woman began, but Principal Allen held up a hand.

"This is a student we're talking about," he said in a stern voice to Miss Clarke.

"Yeah, well he shouldn't be," she said. "Not after what

he did."

"He?" the woman exclaimed. She grabbed at her necklace and started to yank it out from underneath her shirt.

"Yes, Todd is your son, isn't he?" Miss Clarke said.

"Tonya," Todd's mother said. "Her name is Tonya now." In her hand Todd's mother clasped a rainbow talisman she had just pulled out from her shirt. She gripped it tightly, its colors worn and faded together.

Miss Clarke sat back in her chair and folded her arms. "His records still show his name as Todd."

"Which we will fix right away," Principal Allen said apologetically to Todd's parents.

"And it's 'her'," Todd's mother said. "Tonya's preferred pronoun is 'her'."

Miss Clarke rolled her eyes. "I'll be sure to file that information right next to his Hindu caste, his office in the priesthood, and his astrological sign."

Todd's parents looked confused.

"Would you like to also tell me what animal he was last reincarnated from as well?" Miss Clarke asked.

"I don't understand why you're saying that," Todd's mother said, her hand tight around her rainbow talisman. Todd's father pulled his rainbow talisman out as well, mirroring his wife.

"And this," Principal Allen said, raising a finger for attention, "this is what I meant when I said there was more to the story. Miss Clarke, Tonya's mother informed me you have been constantly antagonizing Tonya, refusing to call her by her preferred pronouns, not letting her use the girl's bathroom if girls were inside. In short, you have been misgendering her!"

"Misgendering?" Miss Clarke scowled at Principal

Allen. "Their a-hole of a son pissed all over my desk in full view of my class, and you want to talk to me about 'misgendering'?"

"Because Tonya was provoked!" Todd's mother shouted. "How did you expect her to react? Why don't you tell Principal Allen what you taught in class today?"

Miss Clarke shook her head. "I have no idea what you're talking about. Nothing I said would justify what Todd did."

"What was your lesson on today?" Principal Allen asked.

"Human reproduction."

"Yes!" Todd's mother said. "Which frankly shouldn't be taught anymore given how often it leads to discrimination. And what did you say? What did you say? You said that 'women get pregnant'. That's what you said!"

Miss Clarke raised an eyebrow. "Yes … because that's biology. I'm a biology teacher."

"But not all women are the kind of women that can get pregnant!" Todd's mother said. "Tonya won't be able to! How was she supposed to react to an offensive statement like that?"

"In the first place, maybe the fact that it's biologically impossible for someone like Todd to get pregnant should make you rethink your ridiculous beliefs. But more importantly, how does that justify in anyway what Todd did? He pissed all over my desk! In front of the whole class! I assure you, no one in my class has any doubt now what gender Todd really is."

"Not all girls look like girls," Todd's mother said.

"If Todd doesn't look like a girl, what makes you think he is a girl?"

"Because she told us she is!"

"And that's all it takes? He tells you what you have to believe, and you just believe him? No proof necessary?"

A knock came to the door, and Principal Allen called, "Come in."

The door opened and a middle-aged caucasian man stepped in. Polished shoes, khaki pants, a brown blazer over a blue button-up shirt. He was slightly overweight and had the enlarged face that went with it. He wore small round glasses, and in the center of his forehead, a large eye was painted in bright rainbow colors.

"Please have a seat," Principal Allen said to the man, gesturing at the opposite wall from where Miss Clarke was sitting. Principal Allen then turned to Miss Clarke. "This is Tonya's psychologist. We asked him to join us to help straighten out this matter."

"I don't see the point of bringing a psychologist here," Miss Clarke said. "And why aren't we focusing on what really matters: The outrageous behavior of their son!"

"Tonya is a girl," the psychologist said with authority after he had sat down.

"See!" Todd's mother said to Miss Clarke. "He's a psychologist! He would know!"

"Like I said before. Todd exposed himself to me and my entire class. There's no point in claiming he's a girl. Speaking as a biology teacher, I assure you: Todd is 100% boy."

"Tonya's sex might be male, but she identifies as a girl, which means her gender is a girl, which means that Tonya is a girl," the psychologist said.

"Why in the world should I believe that?" Miss Clarke asked. "Just because he said so? Just because you say so?"

A look of confusion crossed the psychologist's face, who

had never been confronted with that question before and who noticed for the first time that Miss Clarke wasn't holding a rainbow talisman. But he was quickly rescued by Todd's mother, who repeated faithfully, "He's a psychologist. He would know."

And so, reinflated by this statement of faith, the psychologist sat up straight, and said, "Quite right. Now it seems to me that what's causing your confusion is a lack of understanding of the difference between biological sex, which you as a biology teacher are familiar with, and gender, which falls under my domain."

Todd's mother nodded fiercely.

"What in the world are you talking about?" Miss Clarke asked. "The word 'gender' is a synonym for sex! You say gender. I say sex. We're talking about the same thing!"

"Absolutely not," the psychologist responded. "Our sex might be assigned physically, but our gender is something we have to find out for ourselves. It is what we are happiest to be, and what we are happiest to be treated as. Gender is not sex."

"Exactly!" Todd's mother said, holding her rainbow talisman in a fist that she shook with enthusiasm. "He's a psychologist. He would know!"

Miss Clarke snorted. "What makes someone happiest? That's what you want to base reality on? Stop being so absurd. Happiness doesn't define reality. Reality defines reality. And, guess what, sometimes reality sucks, but that's just reality."

"I beg your pardon," the psychologist said.

"And that line of yours that gender is different from sex is the most deceitful pile of — and you know it. So you invent some invisible, imaginary construct, discoverable only by psychologists, a construct you claim is completely different from sex, and then you purposefully choose the word 'gender' to describe it, knowing full well that the word 'gender' is commonly used as a synonym for sex. And do you stop there? No. You take the words"boy" and "girl", "man" and "woman", and you claim them for your imaginary construct as well, again knowing full well that they are used as synonyms for "male" and "female". So why did you do that? If the imaginary construct that you call gender is completely different from sex, then why did you purposefully choose synonyms for sex to name it? Why didn't you choose a completely different word? You could have called it someone's aura. You could have said that Todd has a green aura, and someone else has a blue aura, and someone else has a polka dot one. You could have said that, so why didn't you?"

The psychologist had no response.

"I'll tell you why," Miss Clarke continued. "It's because if you called it something completely different, then everyone would treat it like we treat other religious beliefs we don't believe in: We'd ignore it. And you don't want it to be ignored, do you? Oh no. You want it to be believed. You want to *force* people to believe in it. So what do you do? You steal a synonym for sex, and then you demand that your imaginary construct *overrides* biological sex itself!"

"Now don't be ridiculous," the psychologist said. "That's not what we're saying at all."

"Then why are we even here?" Miss Clarke asked. "We should be here talking about what that little SOB Todd did in my classroom, but, no, apparently we're here because I 'misgendered' him. And what did I do to do that? I'll tell you what I did: I described human reproduction according to the reality of biological sex! I used pronouns based on the reality of biological sex! And so you have your imaginary construct you call gender, which I guess I'll call *psychological*-gender, and we have the real fact of biological sex, let's call that *biological*-gender, and the only reason we're here is because I refuse to let psychological-gender override biological-gender. That's why we're here!"

"That's not it at all," the psychologist said. "Gender is different than biological sex. What we're asking is that you affirm Tonya's gender identity."

"Oh, come on. Stop treating me like I'm an idiot," Miss Clarke said. "That's a complete pile of — and you know it! In one breath you claim that psychological-gender is different than biological-gender, and then in the next you demand that we replace the use of biological-gender with your made-up psychological-gender in every situation we would normally use biological-gender!"

"That's not true at all."

"Oh, please. Let's go through the list. Pronouns: Different pronouns only exist because of biological-gender, now you demand we base them on psychological-gender. Bathrooms: Different bathrooms only exist because of biological-gender, now you demand we base them on psychological-gender. Sports leagues: Different leagues only exist because of biological-gender, now you demand we base them on psychological-gender. Sexual attraction: Different types of sexual attraction only exist because of biological-gender, now you demand we base it on psychological-gender. Shall I go on?"

The psychologist was once again at a loss for words.

"You claim psychological-gender is different than biological-gender," Miss Clarke said, "and then you demand we replace biological-gender with psychological-gender in every case we would normally use it. You deceitful sack of —. What you really want to do is to redefine reality as whatever you want it to be, whatever makes you 'happiest', but when it comes to biological-gender you know you stand no chance to justify your beliefs with proof like science actually requires, so you come up with this BS line that psychological-gender is different than biological-gender and therefore doesn't have to contend against the empirical proof that biological-gender is based on, yet at the same time you demand that psychological-gender should override biological-gender in all cases. To which I say: Absolutely not! Biology is a science. Everything it claims about reality is based on proof, on empirical evidence. When we want to know something about reality, we pull out our microscopes and we *discover* it. We don't sit in our chairs and pick our noses and ask someone what fantasy would make them the happiest and then demand that the whole world *believes* that fantasy."

"I'm not going to just sit here and let you belittle my profession!" the psychologist said.

"How could I belittle your profession more than psychologists like you already have? Seriously, what has happened to psychology? You were supposed to help people come to grips with reality. Did you decide that was too hard and gave up? Because you certainly aren't doing that anymore. My grandfather was a psychologist. He would be ashamed of what his profession has become. But that's because he was a reality-affirming psychologist, not a fantasy-affirming psychologist like so many of you are today."

"That's absolutely not true," the psychologist said. "We help our patients come to grips with the reality of their gender identity."

"Based on what proof?" Miss Clarke said. "What is the proof that gender identity exists and isn't just a fantasy? What is the proof that it is anything more concrete than any other religious belief? What is the proof it's so important we should force the world to let it override the provable reality of biological sex?"

"There have been many, many studies done on this . . . " the psychologist began.

"Psychological studies," Miss Clarke said.

"Well, yes, of course."

"Which means they're completely irrelevant. You are asking the world to let psychological-gender override biological-gender. Well, psychology doesn't have authority over biology, so your psychological studies are completely useless to justify that. Where is your proof, real proof, not 'I talked to my patient a lot and determined this is what makes him happiest' nonsense."

The psychologist squirmed in his seat. "There have also been brain scan studies that have demonstrated evidence for gender identity."

"Great!" Miss Clarke said. "And what does Todd's brain scan show?"

The psychologist just stared back at her, his eyes as vacant as the rainbow eye painted on his forehead, so Miss Clarke turned to Todd's parents.

"If brain scans are proof of gender identity, then surely you got Todd's brain scanned before you decided he was a girl, right?" Miss Clarke said. "Right?"

Todd's parents looked at the floor.

"The science isn't quite there yet," the psychologist explained.

"Ah, then it's strange you brought it up at all, but we'll forget you mentioned it in order to spare you further embarrassment. So tell me then, what is the proof exactly that Todd is a girl?" Miss Clarke turned to Todd's parents, awaiting an answer.

But Todd's mother didn't seem to know what to say. Clutching her rainbow talisman tightly, she avoided looking at Miss Clarke. Finally, she gestured toward the psychologist. "He's a psychologist," she said weakly. "He would know."

"So, it was counseling sessions then, wasn't it?" Miss Clarke said. "That's the proof your son is a girl? Amazing. What science will psychologists override through counseling sessions next? Perhaps they'll discover a new element. Won't chemists be surprised! Or maybe they'll discover there's a black hole hiding behind the sun. Good luck explaining that, physicists and astronomers! Or . . . " Miss Clarke paused before continuing, "or we could come to our senses and acknowledge that psychology doesn't have authority over chemistry, and psychology doesn't have authority over physics or astronomy, and psychology certainly doesn't have authority over biology!"

The psychologist glared at Miss Clarke. Any attempt to use logic or reason stood no chance against someone like her, that was obvious. What mattered was faith, something Miss Clarke clearly lacked. Then the psychologist turned toward Principal Allen and what he saw made him smile. What mattered was faith, yes, and what really mattered was that the authorities had faith; and Principal Allen was sitting there, red faced with anger, staring at Miss Clarke, gripping a rainbow talisman tightly in his hand.

The psychologist turned his smile toward Miss Clarke.

"Did anyone tell you how creepy your smile looks underneath that rainbow eye?" Miss Clarke said, and Principal Allen yelled, "Enough!"

Everyone in the room turned toward him. "I've heard enough of this! All of you can go." He shook a finger at Miss Clarke. "Except you. You will stay."

The psychologist winked at Miss Clarke as he stood up. Let's see how far logic and reason get you now, he thought, smiling as he followed Tonya's parents out of the office. A heated conversation ensued between Miss Clarke and Principal Allen, the voices growing softer the further the psychologist walked from the office, but he heard multiple colorful obscenities from Miss Clarke, and he heard a loud authoritative statement from Principal Allen: "He's a psychologist. He would know."

Because really, what more was there to say?

The psychologist stepped out of the high school out onto the sidewalk. What a glorious day! His spirits had been buoyed up by the intense thanks he had received from Tonya's parents and from his victory in the confrontation with Miss Clarke—thanks to the faith of Principal Allen, and he felt so good he decided to not call a rideshare to return to his office but instead to walk there and enjoy himself along the way.

Taking a right as the quiet residential street came to an end at busy Center Street, he happily lost himself in the crowds of people walking with him or against him along the wide sidewalk. He nodded at the people he passed, always pleased to see them offer him a deferential bow after they noticed his rainbow eye.

A small line of people at a street vendor all bowed in unison, a sign of deference that so delighted him he stopped to understand the crying he heard there.

"But I don't like orange soda. I wanted root beer!" a young boy said to his mother, looking disappointed at the orange drink she had just handed him.

The psychologist turned to the boy's mother. "What seems to be the problem?" he asked.

The woman was paying the street vendor and didn't look at the psychologist as she responded, "Oh, he's just upset they were out of root beer."

"Would he be happier if his soda were root beer?" the psychologist asked.

"Yes, root beer is his favorite," the woman said, returning her credit card to her purse.

"Then it is root beer!" the psychologist said with authority.

The woman laughed without looking up. "Listen, I appreciate you trying to help, but my son is just going to have to learn to live with—" But then she noticed his rainbow eye and froze.

"I'm so sorry," she said. Frantically she pulled her rainbow talisman out and held it tightly. "I didn't realize who I was talking to."

"I understand," the psychologist said. "I'm just happy I was able to straighten it out."

"Of course," the woman said. "Thank you. Thank you so much." Then she turned to her son. "Did you hear what the psychologist said? Your soda is actually root beer! Isn't that wonderful?"

"But it's orange," the boy said, looking at his soda with a scowl on his face.

"No, honey, it's root beer. That's what the psychologist said. He's a psychologist. He would know. Why don't you take a little sip?"

The boy looked dubiously at his mother. Then he took a quick sip. "It's orange!" he wailed.

"No, no," the mother said. "Sometimes root beer just looks and tastes like orange soda. But it's root beer. You have to believe it's root beer!"

"It's not root beer. It's orange!" the boy wailed.

By this point, every person standing in line had pulled out their rainbow talismans, as did a small crowd of onlookers who had stopped to see the commotion. The mother blushed as everyone's stares started to change into glares.

"I'm sorry," she said, dragging her wailing son away. "I'll teach him better. I will!"

The psychologist shook his head. It was tragic when someone refused to accept what would make them happy. He shrugged and turned in the direction of his office once again, his mood quickly returning to his prior cheerfulness.

But his expertise was needed once again on the next block. He had paused to acknowledge a small group of young women in front of an ice cream shop who had all bowed with great reverence to him, when the chocolate ice cream one girl held in her hand fell out of its cone onto the sidewalk.

"Oh no!" she said, half sad, half laughing.

"You're such a klutz,"" her friends laughed cheerfully at her.

"That was quite unfortunate," the psychologist said. "But tell me, would you be happier if you still had ice cream?"

The girl laughed. "Of course."

"Then you do!" the psychologist said with authority. "Your ice cream scoop is still there. It never fell to the ground!"

The girl gave a nervous laugh, but then stopped when he didn't join in. "Wait, you're serious?"

"Your ice cream is right there," the psychologist said, pointing at the empty air above her cone. "Why don't you taste it?"

The girl looked from the psychologist, to her empty cone, and then to her friends, who by now had all pulled out their rainbow talismans. She pulled out her rainbow talisman as well.

"It's good to know you didn't actually drop your ice cream, isn't it?" one of her friends asked, the earlier cheerfulness replaced with a hollow falseness.

"Go ahead and taste your ice cream," the psychologist said, pointing at the empty cone.

The girl flushed red with embarrassment, but she gripped her rainbow talisman tightly in her hand and licked the empty air. "Mmmm," she said unconvincingly. "I love chocolate."

The psychologist smiled in self-satisfaction. "I'm happy to have been of service," he said. Then he nodded and continued on his way.

The next block held no dilemmas for the psychologist to solve, so he found himself waiting at the intersection for the light to change. To his left, the busy traffic of Center Street buzzed past. Suddenly, he felt a pain in his right shin as something crashed into his leg and almost knocked him over.

"Ow!" he yelled in anger, looking down at the bratty tomboy that had run into him with her skateboard. "Watch where you're going!"

The tomboy was twelve, maybe thirteen. She wore a sports jersey and boy's shorts and her short hair was hidden completely by her helmet. "Sorry, mister," she said without even looking up at him. Picking up her skateboard, she rose to her feet and walked over to the other crosswalk, waiting to cross the busy six-lane Center Street.

The psychologist scowled at her, his shin aching.

"Why are you standing there?" he asked the tomboy.

"I'm waiting for the walk sign," the tomboy said.

"But it's blinking right now," the psychologist said, pointing across six lanes of speeding traffic. "Can't you see it?"

The tomboy looked at the pedestrian signal, a red hand clearly visible on the other side of all the passing cars, and then she looked at the psychologist. Her eyes widened when she saw his rainbow eye.

"The walk sign is on," the psychologist said with authority. "There is no traffic. You should cross the street now."

The tomboy looked up at the psychologist's rainbow eye. She looked at the cars and trucks rushing by. She looked at the psychologist's rainbow eye again.

People were stopping now, curious at what was happening. One by one, they pulled out their rainbow talismans.

"He's a psychologist. He would know," one said.

"He's a psychologist. He would know," another agreed.

The tomboy looked again at the busy street. She looked again at the psychologist. She looked at the crowd that had gathered around them.

"He's a psychologist. He would know," a woman carrying a grocery bag said.

"He's a psychologist. He would know," a man in a suit said.

The blood had all drained from the tomboy's face. Slowly she reached into her shirt and pulled out a rainbow talisman. She looked down at it for a moment. Then she looked up at the busy street. Then down at her rainbow talisman again.

"He's a psychologist. He would know," the crowd said.

The tomboy looked up at the psychologist again, her rainbow talisman clutched tightly in her hand. The psychologist give her a sharp nod toward the road.

Gripping her rainbow talisman tightly against her breast, the tomboy closed her eyes and stepped out onto the crosswalk. Three steps later she was hit by a delivery truck going forty miles an hour. There was a bone-crunching thud and a spray of blood followed by a squeal of brakes as the tomboy's body flew dozens of feet down the street, bouncing and skidding, a trail of blood and gore smeared onto the pavement behind her until her body finally slid to a halt.

The air filled with screams. The truck had stopped and the driver was getting out. People were running toward the tomboy's body.

The psychologist shook his head with annoyance. Lifting his hands high into the air he shouted, "Stop!"

Everyone froze and turned to look at him.

"What are you doing?" he asked. Then he paused to wipe some blood from his cheek.

"There was no accident," he continued. "There is no body. There is nothing to see, nothing to be upset about."

The crowd looked at the tomboy's motionless body. Then they looked at the psychologist's rainbow eye. Then they looked at the tomboy's body again. Slowly, one by one, they pulled out their rainbow talismans.

The psychologist nodded. "There was no accident," he repeated. "There is no body. There never was a tomboy at all."

He pointed at his rainbow eye. "I'm a psychologist. I would know."

Provable Reality, Cold and Indifferent

Provable reality is cold and indifferent. It doesn't care about your happiness, your mental health, or what makes you more or less likely to commit suicide. Provable reality simply is. It doesn't care about you at all, or about me, or about anyone else. As content to rule over a barren rock drifting silently in the void of space as it is to reign over a warm planet teeming with life and intelligence, provable reality simply doesn't care.

Warmth, love, mercy; purpose and meaning—seek those elsewhere. But if you want that which holds sway in our secular neutrality, that which all can be compelled to accept, then you have met your cold mistress; acquaint yourself with her indifferent grip.

Converting the Two-Spirit

Dr. Herbert shook her head slowly from side to side as she read her receptionist's note about her next appointment. She did her best to not scowl, but the sides of her mouth seemed to drop of their own accord.

"Concerned about daughter's gender identity."

She willed her scowl to go away, but it simply wouldn't budge. Parents like this enraged her to no end. Concerned about their daughter's gender identity? Well, she was concerned about their parenting skills! Didn't they understand how important gender identity was? Didn't they understand they had a duty to affirm their child's beliefs, whatever they might be?

And if they were "concerned", that probably meant they wanted her to help change it. Didn't they know that was illegal?

The fact was some people just shouldn't be parents, Dr. Herbert thought. There should be a license required, and one of the requirements for that license should be an acceptance and support of gender identity. If a person wanted to be backwards and bigoted, then let them do so alone, with their children safely removed from their home by child services.

Her thoughts were interrupted by a knock at her door. Dr. Herbert sighed and swiveled her seat away from the computer and toward the chairs in the center of her office. Steeling herself to face the conservative neanderthals, she hid her scowl and said, "Come in."

The door opened and three people walked in, an adult man and woman followed by a teenage girl. They were all white, which somehow matched Dr. Herbert's negative preconceptions of them perfectly. The woman was stocky and the man quite large. He had the look of an ex-jock, Dr. Herbert thought, which made her dislike him even more. The two adults were dressed in business casual, their polo shirts tucked into slacks, making them look like they'd come straight from a Republican convention. The teenager followed a few steps behind them, her long blond hair spilling over the shoulders of a trendy band's t-shirt. She had her arms folded tightly and a death glare fixed at her parents' backs.

The trio sat down, the girl between her parents, and the room settled into an awkward silence, which Dr. Herbert had no intention of breaking. She liked to force her patients to begin the conversation. It was a good way to understand the power dynamics in a relationship. She was surprised when the woman, instead of the man, started talking.

"Thank you for meeting with us," the woman said. "My name is Monica, and this is my husband, Peter." She gestured toward the man sitting on the other side of their daughter. "And this is Cassidy," she said, pointing at the teenage girl.

"I'm happy to meet you," Dr. Herbert lied. "Now please tell me why we're here?" She already knew, of course, but she refused to be the one to say it.

"It's Cassidy's gender identity," Monica said.

"Okay," Dr. Herbert said, doing her best to not scowl. "And why do you want to talk about Cassidy's gender identity?"

"Because it's wrong," Monica said, "and we need help convincing her it's wrong. You see—"

But Dr. Herbert cut her off with an upraised hand. "Let's stop right here," she said. "I want to make it clear that the American Psychological Association has an official position that attempting to change a child's gender identity is harmful to them. And, I'll add, it's actually illegal in this state for a therapist to try."

"But you don't understand," Monica began.

"Oh, I understand completely," Dr. Herbert said. "I understand that if you have a problem with your daughter's gender identity, then the problem lies with you."

"No," Monica said. "You don't understand. Let me explain—"

"There's nothing to explain," Dr. Herbert said. "A person's gender identity is an innate part of themselves. Asking your daughter to change her gender identity would be like asking her to cut off her arm. It can't be changed, and it's wrong for you to even think that it should be."

Exasperated, Monica threw up her arms. "But she identifies as a two-spirit!"

Dr. Herbert froze. She looked at Cassidy, at white, white Cassidy.

"Oh . . . " she said, ". . . well that's different."

"That's what I've been trying to tell you!" Monica said. "If she identified as a boy or as non-binary or as anything really, we'd be totally fine with it. But we're white. We don't have a drop of Native American blood in us, yet she claims to be a two-spirit."

Dr. Herbert turned to Cassidy. Speaking softly, she said, "Cassidy, do you understand why it's wrong for you to identify as a two-spirit?"

"No," Cassidy said, defiantly.

"Cassidy, you're white," Dr. Herbert said. "And the two-spirit gender identity is only for Native Americans. It's part of their religious culture. It's a Native American belief that someone has both a male spirit and a female spirit inside their body. When you identify as a two-spirit, you are stealing their culture. It's cultural appropriation, and that's really wrong for a white person to do."

"You're talking about it as if it were my choice," Cassidy said. "But I *am* a two-spirit. That's my gender identity. Are you trying to tell me I should change my gender identity?"

"Maybe there are other ways you could express it," Dr. Herbert said. "Why not call yourself non-binary, or gender-fluid? Wouldn't that be close enough?"

Cassidy shook her head. "Those aren't my gender identity. I'm a two-spirit, someone with both a male spirit and a female spirit inside them. That's what I am."

"But only Native Americans can be two-spirits," Dr. Herbert said.

"I know," Cassidy said. "So, since I'm a two-spirit, that means I'm a Native American."

Dr. Herbert was taken aback. "Wait," she said. "I thought your mother said you didn't have a drop of Native American blood in you?"

"That's right," Monica said, nodding. "All our ancestors are from Europe."

"Cassidy," Dr. Herbert said, "you can't just claim to be Native American. That's not reality. And since you're not Native American, that means you can't be a two-spirit."

"But I don't have XY chromosomes," Cassidy said, "yet that wouldn't stop me from identifying as a boy, would it?"

"Well, no," Dr. Herbert said.

"So not having Native American DNA can't stop me from being a two-spirit either," Cassidy said. "Either gender identity trumps DNA or it doesn't."

"See, this is what she does," Peter said, speaking for the first time. "She keeps twisting us up with logic."

Dr. Herbert smiled sympathetically at Peter. What a good, conscientious man, she thought. "I know you're doing your best," she told him. Then she paused for a moment to think before turning back to Monica. "Usually in situations like this we just let social shaming take care of the problem."

"We've tried," Monica said. "All of her friends rejected her weeks ago, and we've been encouraging her teachers to call her a bigot to her face, but nothing is working."

"Hmm," Dr. Herbert said. "Do you think maybe she doesn't understand why cultural appropriation is so wrong? Maybe she hasn't woken up to her white privilege?"

Monica held up her hands helplessly. "We're doing everything we can. We've been making her repeat the anti-whiteness affirmation I learned in college to herself in the mirror every morning, but I don't think it's helping."

Dr. Herbert turned back to Cassidy. "Could you tell me the affirmation you repeat every morning?"

Cassidy rolled her eyes and spoke in a monotone voice, "I hate my white skin. It is the ugliest thing in the entire world. Everything bad that has ever happened and everything bad that will ever happen is my white skin's fault. I could spend my entire life trying to atone for the sins of my white skin, and it wouldn't be enough. I hate my white skin."

Dr. Herbert clapped. "That's wonderful. But, Cassidy, I wonder if you're paying attention to the words?"

Cassidy shrugged.

"Given all the privilege you get from your white skin, can't you see how wrong it is to steal something from a marginalized culture like Native Americans? Can't you see that it's wrong for you to claim to be a two-spirit?"

"Can't *you* see that you're misgendering me?" Cassidy said. "Isn't misgendering wrong too?"

"Yes, misgendering is also wrong," Dr. Herbert said. "But don't you think there are degrees of wrongness? Like rape is wrong—it's horrible really—but murder is still worse, right?"

Cassidy smirked. "So, what you're saying is it's okay for you to rape me because at least it isn't as bad as murder?"

"Yes," Dr. Herbert said. "Wait, no! That's not the way I wanted it to sound."

Peter spoke, "Maybe it's more like a misdemeanor versus a felony?"

"No, no," Dr. Herbert said. "I think it's best if we move away from crime analogies."

Cassidy chuckled.

"Do you see?" Monica said to Dr. Herbert, pointing at Cassidy. "What are we supposed to do? Social shaming doesn't work, and any time we try to reason with her, she ties us up in knots. But we can't have her keep claiming to be a two-spirit. That's just wrong."

Dr. Herbert leaned back in her chair, folded her arms, and studied Cassidy.

"Yes," she said. "This is a difficult problem." She pondered the situation for another moment. "Perhaps it would be appropriate to take a ... less standard approach."

At these words, Cassidy's gaze fixed on Dr. Herbert's face, Cassidy's eyes alert and attentive.

"Cassidy," Dr. Herbert began slowly. "Can you prove that you're a two-spirit?"

"I identify as a two-spirit," Cassidy said. "And my gender identity is innate and only knowable by myself. That proves that I'm a two-spirit."

"Does it though?" Dr. Herbert asked. "You're clearly a very logical person, so let's be logical about this. A two-spirit is a part of Native American culture. It's something that only Native Americans can be. Yet, you claim to identify as a two-spirit, and you claim that that *makes* you a two-spirit and therefore makes you a Native American."

"Right," Cassidy said. "Go on."

"But whether or not you are Native American is part of reality," Dr. Herbert said.

"Just like whether I am a girl or a boy," Cassidy said.

"Yes, but let's not get distracted here," Dr. Herbert said. "My point is this: Whether or not you are a Native American is part of reality. And each of us have an equal right to determine what reality is, don't we?"

"I guess so," Cassidy said.

"But when you claim that your gender identity is a two-spirit, and you claim that reality itself should be determined by your identity, can't you see the privileged position you place yourself in? Can't you see what power you are claiming over your parents and over everyone else?"

"Please explain," Cassidy said.

"Let's just imagine that gender identity didn't exist," Dr. Herbert said. "Now, in that world, how would you decide if someone was Native American or not?"

"By their DNA, I guess."

"Right, by real physical proof. And that's something that I could verify, right? And your mother could. And your father."

"I guess so."

"So in this imaginary world where gender identity didn't exist, all of us would have an equal ability to determine whether someone is Native American or not."

"Or a boy or a girl."

"Right, but then you introduce gender identity, and you claim that you identify as a two-spirit, and you claim that your gender identity is more important than the physical proof itself. But think about what that does to everyone else. Can your mother verify your gender identity?"

"No."

"Can your father?"

"No."

"Who can?"

"Just me."

"So, what you're asking is for everyone else, everyone in the entire world, to give up their right to determine what reality is and instead to defer that decision entirely to you. Can't you see what a privileged position you are claiming for yourself? Can't you see how much power you are demanding over others? Power to define reality itself! Now tell me, Cassidy, do you think it's fair for someone to demand that much power over the whole world?"

"I guess not," Cassidy said. "So what are you asking me to do?"

Dr. Herbert paused, noticing how intently all three of them were waiting for her next words. She tried to choose them perfectly. "What I'm asking you to do," she said, "is to be fair. What I'm asking you to do is to check your privilege. I'm asking you to give up this unfair power you have demanded over others and to return to an equal ground with everyone else. And the way to do that is to return to what is actually provable. Not just what you personally claim to be the truth, but what you can actually prove to be the truth."

"And what does that mean about my gender identity?" Cassidy asked. "Are you saying I should ... change it?"

"Well, what gender can you actually prove you are? What does your DNA say?"

"That I'm a girl," Cassidy said. "So you're saying I should change my gender identity to match what my body proves my gender is?"

"Yes," Dr. Herbert said. "In this case, I think it's for the best."

"And you're helping me make that change? You're counseling me and guiding me to change my gender identity from a two-spirit to a girl?"

"Yes, I hope what I said will help you accept that you are a girl."

Monica and Peter both turned questioning looks to Cassidy, who nodded. "Okay, that should be enough," she said to them. "Arrest her."

Dr. Herbert grabbed the arms of her chair. "Wait, what?"

Cassidy stood. She pulled her hair back into a ponytail and put on glasses, the "teenage girl" replaced by a woman years older. Monica and Peter rose to their feet as well. Monica displayed a police badge to Dr. Herbert while Peter lifted her to her feet.

"You have the right to remain silent," Peter began as he placed Dr. Herbert's hands behind her back and handcuffed them.

"I don't understand what's happening!" Dr. Herbert

said.

"... you have the right to an attorney ..." Peter continued.

"Why are you doing this?" Dr. Herbert asked. "What did I do wrong?"

"You know quite well that it's illegal for a therapist to try to change someone's gender identity," Cassidy said.

"What?" Dr. Herbert said. "But that law was only supposed to apply to conservatives! It wasn't supposed to apply to people like me. I have good intentions!"

Cassidy shrugged. "The law is the law."

"But it was cultural appropriation!" Dr. Herbert said.

The three officers didn't respond. They started walking Dr. Herbert out of her office.

"It was cultural appropriation!" Dr. Herbert repeated. "How could you expect me to ignore that? You shouldn't be arresting me. You should be thanking me. It was cultural appropriation! White people can't be two-spirits! It isn't allowed!"

There Is No Valid Proof of Gender Identity, And There Never Will Be

While I am glad journalists are highlighting the flaws in psychological studies about gender identity and I view this as valuable work and am happy it's being done, I am taking a different tack here. Because even if every one of these studies were executed flawlessly and even if the results they claimed to reach were accurate, those results still would not justify the way psychologists are trying to use them. My argument is simple: It is impossible for psychology to prove that the "gender" of gender identity is real.

Gender identity believers declare that "gender is different than sex" and that our gender identity is our inner sense of what our "gender" is and represents something innate and immutable about ourselves, something core to our being as a person. But what exactly is this "gender" they are speaking of? It isn't helpful to provide their definition because their definition of the word often doesn't match the way they actually use it, so let me try to describe it. We start with our physical body. Okay, that's obvious. We can see it. We can touch it. It's material. It's provably there. Now imagine an incorporeal *something* around that physical body, an aura, a manifestation of a human soul, a twirly mist, something immaterial, something transcendental. And this transcendental gender that surrounds each of us, so its believers claim, has a masculine or feminine aspect to it, or both, or neither, or something entirely unrelated to masculine/feminine. And our gender identity is our internal sense of what that transcendental gender is.

But here's the thing: transcendental gender doesn't exist. It doesn't exist in the same way that dragons, and vampires, and werewolves don't exist. It isn't actually there. Gender identity is an internal sense of nothing. What it's identifying isn't real.

The thoughts are there, yes. The beliefs are there, yes. The internal sense is there, yes, the *wish*, the *fantasy*, the *preference*. But this is not the type of thing that can be considered part of provable reality because this is not the type of thing that is actually *provable*. Gender identity is simply a personal belief, not worthy of any more recognition or protection than any other personal belief, and it is impossible for psychology to prove otherwise.

What Psychology Actually Claims

If you pay attention to the claims that psychological studies make in favor of gender identity or "gender" surgeries, you'll note they never actually claim to *prove* that the "gender" which gender identity is supposedly identifying actually exists. They only focus on the *effect* that treating that belief as true has on the mental health of their patients.

Consider some examples:

"Pubertal Suppression for Transgender Youth and Risk

of Suicidal Ideation" (AAP, 2020)

> After adjustment for demographic variables and level of family support for gender identity, those who received treatment with pubertal suppression, when compared with those who wanted pubertal suppression but did not receive it, had lower odds of lifetime suicidal ideation

Does "lower odds of lifetime suicidal ideation" prove that "gender" exists? No.

"Well-being and suicidality among transgender youth after gender-affirming hormones" (APA, 2019)

> After gender-affirming hormones, a significant increase in levels of general well-being and a significant decrease in levels of suicidality were observed.

Does "a significant increase in levels of general well-being" prove that "gender" exists? No.

"A Systematic Review of the Psychological Benefits of Gender-Affirming Surgery" ("Considerations in Gender Reassignment Surgery, An Issue of Urologic Clinics", 2019)

> Most of the studies included in this review indicate that GAS lead to multiple, significant psychological benefits among individuals with gender dysphoria

Does "significant psychological benefits" prove that "gender" exists? No.

Psychology never makes the claim it can directly demonstrate that "gender" exists in a real, objective sense because the field of psychology is incapable of making such measurements. If there actually is a transcendental gender, it would have to be discovered by a new field of science with new instruments capable of measuring whatever this "gender" people believe in is actually composed of.

Instead, psychologists run tests where they treat a certain belief as true, including medical intervention to prevent the natural disproof from manifesting itself (e.g. puberty blockers and surgical modifications). And then they tell us that treating a belief as true had a positive impact on their patient's mental health, which apparently means we're supposed to treat the belief as true?

Were you aware that this is how reality was being decided by our society? Do you, like me, live in a secular society? Is this how you expected your secular society decided what is real? That we were deciding *reality itself* based on what specific privileged people claim makes them happier? I'm assuming this is surprising to you, hopefully shocking, yet this is the demand being made of us by the American Psychological Association, the American Medical Association, the American Academy of Pediatrics, etc. All supposedly secular organizations, all currently acting in a very anti-secular way.

Biological Sex Is a Physical Category

Let's be clear about what is at stake here: biological sex is a physical category. This isn't some abstract concept. This is an actual material category within the material world. Consider how our biological sex is determined. Is it based on identity? Is it based on what makes us happiest? No, it's based on proof. We don't decide what sex we are. Reality decides it for us. In most cases, all it takes is a basic observation of someone's anatomy. But even in the rare cases of physical defect, observations can be made of an individual's DNA, etc; and in all cases, the determination is made based on proof.

There is a sub-genre of gender identity apologetics that goes something like this: "Biological sex is complicated, so complicated, you wouldn't believe how complicated. In fact let me go multiple pages telling you how much more complicated it is than you ever imagined", and then they throw in at the end "and that's why everyone should believe in gender identity!" It's amusing to read these non sequiturs because they completely miss the point. It doesn't matter how simple or complicated biological sex is to determine. The only thing that matters is that it is determined based on *proof.* If it can be proven you have this set of physical characteristics, you are a male. If it can be proven you have these other physical characteristics, you are a female.

Gender Identity Is Overriding Biological Sex

And because biological sex is determined based on proof, it is rightfully considered part of our society's shared reality, which means we structure things around it. We build separate bathrooms based on biological sex, and separate prisons. We create separate sports leagues. We have different pronouns, one per sex, and we structure our language and communication about sexual attraction based on this physical category.

But then believers in gender identity come along and

demand that biological sex be overridden by gender identity. They demand that bathrooms be determined by gender identity, not sex. They demand that prisons be based on gender identity, not sex. They demand that sports leagues be based on gender identity, not sex. They demand that pronouns be based on gender identity, not sex. They demand that sexual attraction be based on gender identity, not sex.

And remember, the "gender" of gender identity doesn't exist! We have all these ways our society has shaped itself around the provable reality of biological sex, and gender identity—a belief in something that doesn't even exist!—is being allowed to override it.

Claims of Happiness Do Not Prove Reality

One might ask, where have we gone wrong? I think it stems from a lost understanding of how a secular society is supposed to determine its shared reality. At some point along the way, people started thinking that for something to be secular it just has to not come from an organized religion. Well, gender identity doesn't come from an organized religion, does that mean it's secular? To many today, the answer is yes, and that is the problem.

Secular does not mean non-religion. Secular means non-faith. In other words, secular means provable. This is not an attack on religion. I am a religious man, and I don't mean in a cultural sense, I mean in an "I believe in things that contradict provable reality" sense. But what right do I have to force people to treat something as true that I cannot prove to be true? That is why a secular society bases its shared reality solely on proof. That way no one is forced to treat the personal beliefs of others as true. If personal beliefs are claimed as religious, then religious accommodation can be provided for them, but nonbelievers always have the right to not treat unprovable beliefs as true.

Yet somewhere along the way, psychology got the strange idea that reality can be proven through human happiness. Now, to a religious person, this might not sound like such a bad idea at first. Don't you believe that your religion makes you happier, and isn't that part of the reason why you believe in it? But the obvious problem is manifest as soon as you look outside yourself and notice that the world is full of people made happy by beliefs that contradict yours. Furthermore, the beliefs that make you happy might make someone else unhappy.

Part of the problem is there is no way to objectively measure happiness, and there is always the obvious question of "But *should* that make you happy?", which a secular society cannot answer. But a larger problem for psychologists is they are focusing solely on the patient in front of them and forgetting that the universe does not revolve around their patient. Other people exist, and our happiness matters too.

Imagine if you wanted to decide if husbands should be expected to do the dishes or not. So you interview every husband in the world and ask them, "Would it make you happier if your wife always did the dishes?" Unsurprisingly, your study comes back with a resounding "Yes!" And so, following the pattern that psychology is following today, you declare: "Husbands are happier when their wives do the dishes, so wives should always do the dishes."

If you are a woman, I trust you can see the flaw in this reasoning, and I hope all men can too: What about the wives' happiness? Don't they matter too? Of course they do, which is why deciding whether or not husbands should do the dishes, based solely on the "happiness" of the husbands, is not a just way to decide things.

So too with gender identity. Jim, a male, believes he is a woman. Psychology claims that treating him like a woman will improve his mental health. But treating a male like a woman will harm the mental health of Mary and Sara, who don't want males in female bathrooms or dressing rooms; and it will harm the mental health of Laura, who is an athlete who wants the ability to compete solely against females; and it will harm the mental health of David, who doesn't want to be expected to be attracted to other males.

And this is why determining reality based on happiness is unjust. How do you weigh the competing claims of happiness against each other? Yes, I understand it would be convenient for you to say, "Treating Jim like a woman *shouldn't* make these people unhappy", but it does. What are you going to do, send them to reeducation camps? The only recourse is what we are witnessing today: Some people are elevated into the status of a demigod, whose happiness is so important that the rest of us are expected to base reality itself around them, and those who object are dehumanized, thereby justifying why their happiness doesn't matter. Because what does it matter if a "bigot" or a "transphobe" or a "hateful TERF" is unhappy?

Furthermore, human happiness isn't a reliable measurement of reality anyway because between human emotion and reality lies a human, whose personal beliefs and overall emotional resilience can make them more or less capable of dealing with a reality that at times, frankly, sucks; therefore, the fact that a person is happy or sad, stable or suicidal, doesn't prove that the underlying reality is good or bad. Instead, it could simply be that that person hasn't developed a healthy way to deal with reality.

Imagine there are four soldiers whose Humvee is hit by an IED. Two of the soldiers tragically lose their legs, but two leave the accident relatively unharmed. Now imagine ten years later the four soldiers are given a psychological exam where they are asked to describe their emotional state as a consequence of that tragedy. Afterward, a psychologist is given just the self-report of their emotional state. Could that psychologist use their self-report to accurately identify which of the soldiers lost their legs and which didn't? No, they couldn't. It might be that one or both of the soldiers who lost their legs would nevertheless have a more positive emotional state than one or both who didn't. Why? Because their personal beliefs and emotional resilience make them better able to deal with a tragic reality. How then can psychologists use a human's emotional state to prove the existence of an unseen reality? They can't. There is no way for them to distinguish between a supposed unseen reality and a human's response to reality. The fact that a person feels distress, even extreme distress, about reality does not prove there is an unseen reality that is causing their reaction. Instead, they simply might not have the tools or the state of mind to appropriately deal with a reality that they deeply wish were different.

When psychologists demand that reality itself be based on what they claim makes their patients happy, they are not making a rational argument. They are making an anti-secular emotional plea.

"Identity" Is Not a Magic Ticket Around the Burden of Proof

At this point, some might try to work around the unprovability of gender identity by saying something like, "But it's an identity!" as if that makes a difference. But calling something an identity is not a magic ticket around the burden of proof. To say "I identify as" means the same thing as "My personal belief is that I am". This is obvious when you consider that one person's identity can contradict another person's identity. It is not possible to determine reality in this way.

To demonstrate: I self-identify as a human with the sufficient wisdom to determine whether or not someone else's identity is part of provable reality. This identity of mine is based on an internal sense of who I am as a person and is critically important to me. And using this wisdom, which I identify as having, I have determined that gender identity is not part of provable reality.

My own identity, therefore, contradicts the identity of those who claim to identify as a "gender", which demonstrates that using identity as a way to determine reality requires you to pick whose identity to prioritize and whose identity to deprioritize, the same problem seen when trying to determine reality based on happiness.

Nothing Based on Self-Identity Can Be Considered Immutable

As an aside, gender identity believers will often claim that our gender identity is immutable, but how in the world can they know that? To know if something is immutable, you have to be able to have an accurate measurement of it in the past, and in the present, and the ability to have an accurate measurement of it in the future. Only then can you prove that it never changes. But gender identity relies entirely on self-identity. There is no objective way to measure it. And we know for a fact that people's self-identity changes. The drastic cases are those of detransitioners, whose self-identity of "being" transgender was taken so seriously that doctors literally modified their bodies because of it, yet these individuals later realized they made a horrible mistake. Their self-identity *changed.* And even within those who continue to believe they are transgender, you will find a history of their self-identity changing from one "gender" to another. So which one is the "immutable" gender identity and which ones are the wrong ones, and how are we supposed to know the difference?

For this reason, if something is based on self-identity, it cannot be considered to be immutable.

Psychology Has No Right to Expect People To Affirm

My final point about psychology and gender identity is that psychologists are asking things of people that they have no right to ask. To show what I mean, let's consider an extreme hypothetical about the plight of "incels", which is short for "involuntary celibates". These are men who would like to have sex with women but are unable to because woman are not attracted to them. Certainly this would have negative effects on the mental health of these unfortunate men. Suppose a group of psychologists did a study where they first interviewed incels and verified the poor state of their mental health. Then, seeking a solution to improve their patients' mental health, they declared that for the next month all women were required to sexually submit to them: If an incel approached a woman, any woman, and demanded something sexually from her, she was required to consent to it. Now imagine after that hellish month for women that the psychologists sat down with the incels and interviewed them again about their mental health. Is there any doubt that the incels would report it had greatly improved? Half of the human race had been forced to submit to their every desire. They had been treated like demigods! Is there any question that they would report being "happier" because of it?

But who cares if that would make incels happier or not? What about the rights of women! Women are not just the means to improving the mental health of incels. Women, like all humans, are ends in themselves. Psychologists have no right to demand we prioritize someone else's mental health over our own rights. But that is what they are doing with gender identity. We have a secular right to not treat unprovable beliefs as true. Yet psychologists are demanding that we "affirm" their patients' gender identities (treat them as true), claiming that doing so improves their patients' mental health. But any mental health improvement for their patients is irrelevant because they are asking something that they have no right to ask. The universe does not revolve around their patients. Other people exist too, and we are just as important as their patients are. We are not just the means to improving the mental health of psychologists' patients. We are ends in ourselves. Psychology needs to stop expecting things of people it has no right to expect.

Using Brain Scans for Religious Apologetics

We now come to brain scans, which are often claimed to be proof of gender identity without any attention paid to what the research is actually saying and without considering why the research is not being used as the proof it claims to be. So let's talk about science versus religious apologetics. What's the difference? I would say that one difference is the manner in which they move from evidence to conclusion. Science ideally works from the bottom up. Evidence is gathered and based on that evidence, hypotheses are formed, which are tested and replaced if the evidence doesn't match them. In the end we arrive at a theory, which represents the best understanding we have of the evidence to date, yet if new evidence arrives that contradicts that theory, then the theory will be discarded and we will work once again from the bottom, trying to make sense of what Nature is telling us about reality.

Now contrast that with religious apologetics, which works from the top down. With religious apologetics, there is no need to arrive at a theory based on the underlying evidence because the "truth" is already known. Evidence is not sought to disprove this "truth" because that is not the goal of religious apologetics. It is working from the top down. It's not interested in what Nature has to say. It's only interested in gathering nuggets of compatible evidence, never enough to actually reach the supposed "truth" from the bottom up, but sufficient to make believers comfortable in believing it. A key point about religious apologetics is that the "truth" is never actually in danger of being disproven. Any disproof will simply be ignored. In other words, the evidence that is cited as proof of a "truth" would never be accepted as disproof if it had gone the other way.

Using brain scans today to claim proof of gender identity is an example of religious apologetics. The claims are inevitably a discussion of averages. These people, on average, have this characteristic. These people do not, etc. This type of evidence would never have arrived at a theory of an unseen "gender" if people were working from the bottom up, but people are working from the top down. They already have "truth". They are just looking for compatible evidence. And whatever they put forward as evidence would never be accepted as disproof. If it was, then why are brain scans not treated as disproof of gender identity today?

It isn't possible to identify an individual's gender identity based on a brain scan. You can say, oh, this person falls within the averages, etc, but that raises the point: Don't some people fall outside of the averages? And if they do, why isn't that considered disproof of their gender identity? The reason is obvious: It's because we aren't dealing with science here. We're dealing with religious apologetics.

Let's examine this point a little more. If brain scans actually are proof of gender identity, then why are they not being used to actually prove an individual's gender identity? Consider the drastic steps that are taken on behalf of gender identity: People are literally modifying their bodies because of this. Women's breasts are being cut off. Genitalia are being deformed, shaped into insufficient approximations of the opposite sex. And people at times deeply regret this. They believed at one point that they were a different "gender", they modified their bodies because of that belief, and later as they consider the irreversible damage they have done to themselves, they deeply, deeply regret their decision.

Well, if brain scans are proof of gender identity, then why are they not used prior to surgery to prove that surgery is actually needed? If a man believes he is a woman, why isn't his brain scan examined to verify that he actually is a woman? Once again, the reason is obvious: If his brain scan were examined, there is a chance his results would fall outside of what is supposedly "proof" of him being a woman. In other words, his brain scan would disprove his gender identity, and that is a possibility that believers in gender identity will not allow to happen.

Gender Identity Believers Have the Burden of Proof

Gender identity believers claim there is an incorporeal "gender", something that is an immutable part of us, something that is more important to us than even our biological sex, yet something that we cannot see or measure in any way. Well, the burden of proof is on them. If they want that to be believed, they have to prove it is true. Otherwise the default answer is that "gender" doesn't exist.

Keep this in mind whenever proof of gender identity is claimed through brain scans. What is the default answer for the assembled evidence? The default answer is that "gender" doesn't exist, so if there is a reasonable explanation for the results that doesn't involve an invisible "gender", then that conclusion is the correct one, and with brain scans this means that the more likely conclusion is that we are looking at evidence of personal belief, not evidence of reality.

In other words, we are looking at either the result of personal belief inside the brain or else the cause of personal belief. To demonstrate what I mean, consider the case of reincarnation. Suppose an objective correlation in people's brains is discovered that 100% matches a person's belief that their last incarnation was as a deer. Would that prove that reincarnation is true and that that person actually lived their life previously as a deer? Obviously not. I trust that if you don't believe in reincarnation, you will naturally start with the assumption that it isn't true. Any discovered correlation between brain scans and truth claims about previous incarnations would therefore be treated as proof of one's *personal belief*, not proof of an objective fact about reality. In other words, objective criteria in brain scans like this could be used to demonstrate that someone *believed* this about themselves, but they could not be used to prove that their belief was *true*.

For this reason, it is impossible to use brain scans to provide proof of a "gender" that doesn't correspond to male or female. Concepts such as non-binary or two-spirit cannot be proven through brain scans because it is impossible to distinguish between whether someone actually *is* that "gender" or if someone simply *believes* they are that "gender". And since the burden of proof is on gender identity believers, they will never be able to prove that their belief is true through brain scans.

A Male/Female Brain Would Not Prove that "Gender" Exists

Lastly, let's consider the claim that a person's brain can be objectively proven to be a "male brain" or a "female brain" and that a male who believes he is a woman can be proven to have a "female brain" and that a female who believes she is a man can be proven to have a "male brain".

To really understand the implications of treating this claim as true, let's consider two scenarios:

Imagine a female, who agrees that her gender is female, gets a brain scan and its results fall within the averages claimed to be a "male brain". Does that prove she is a transgender even though she believes she isn't? Does that prove, despite both her physical body and her own beliefs, that she is actually a man?

Now imagine a male, who believes his "gender" is female, gets a brain scan and its results fall within the averages of what is claimed to be a "male brain". Does that prove that he *isn't* a transgender? Does that prove he is actually a man, despite believing he is a woman?

If you claim that brain scans are proof of "gender", but you aren't willing to treat them as disproof when they contradict someone's gender identity, then it's obvious you're simply engaging in religious apologetics. You already have your belief, and you won't allow it to be disproven.

In order to actually claim that a male can have a "female brain", you would have to be able to identify specific objective criteria that match 100% with all females that believe their "gender" is female *and* all males that believe their "gender" is female. If even one person falls outside that criteria, then you have not actually discovered proof of a "female brain" that can be used in the way you want to use it. Furthermore, you would have to demonstrate that this criteria is not something that is effected by, for example, injecting a male with female hormones or other influences from the environment.

But let's say that impossible task is reached. What

then? If there comes a time when we can actually prove that a specific male has a "female brain", would that prove the existence of "gender"? Absolutely not. Once again, would having a "female brain" be proof that one actually *is* a female, or would it be proof that one *believes* they are female? In other words, everyone that has a brain like this will believe they are female, but does that make them female?

In the end, the argument ends up becoming one based on happiness. If someone has a "female brain", then it could be argued that they'd be happier living their life as a woman. But does that obligate the rest of the world to treat this male as a woman? No, it doesn't. If the proof says that this is a male with a "female brain", then the reality is that this is a male with a "female brain". In other words: he is still a male.

The very, very best case that could be made by gender identity believers should this unlikely situation arise is that the physical category of biological sex should be expanded to include the brain, thereby transforming a male with a "female brain" from a transgender into someone with an intersex defect. But this expansion of the physical category of biological sex would not be required. We as a society would have to decide whether to do so or not. On one side would be claims of human happiness: "It would make them happier to be treated based on their brain than their body." On the other side would be arguments about the purpose of biological sex and its role in human reproduction. I know which way I would argue. Regardless, this development would be the end of belief in "gender" because at this point we would all be arguing based on proof, with self-identified gender identity left completely in the past.

Secular Compassion for Personal Beliefs

How is it that secular societies have found themselves entangled in such irrational knots regarding gender identity? Why is it so hard to simply say "No" when we are asked to define reality based on what people claim makes them happy? I think in large part it comes down to human compassion and a misunderstanding of how that compassion should be shown by a secular society.

There is no doubt that many people legitimately believe in gender identity. Their willingness to carve up their own bodies is evidence of this fact. When someone believes something so deeply, and when the friction between their personal beliefs and reality causes obvious emotional pain, it is understandable, even expected, to feel compassion toward them. But consider the minority religions within your society. In my case this would include Muslims, Buddhists, and Sikhs, among others. These people believe something deeply as well. Don't you feel compassion for them too? Shouldn't you feel the same degree of compassion toward them as you feel toward those who believe they are a different "gender" than their biological sex?

Yet we are able to show compassion to minority religions without actually treating their beliefs as true. Why is that? It's because they have chosen the correct path to receive secular compassion for their personal beliefs: religious freedom. Muslims are not asking us to treat the truth claims of Islam as true. Sikhs are not demanding we shape our definition of reality around what they believe. The only thing they are asking is to be given an appropriate amount of space for them to live as if their beliefs were true. This is what religious freedom provides, and it provides it while simultaneously protecting the rights of nonbelievers.

A secular state *cannot* treat religious beliefs as true, and it therefore cannot expect nonbelieving citizens to do so either.

And so we reach the problem: Those who believe in gender identity are not taking the path of religious freedom. They are claiming that their beliefs aren't religious at all. As a result, it might appear that the only way to show compassion to them is to bend reality on their behalf. But that is a false choice. We do not have to limit ourselves to either violating secular neutrality (by bending reality) or to not providing compassion for personal beliefs. The path of religious freedom is always open, whether a person is willing to take it or not. Continuing to point them toward that path is a display of compassion, and it is the only legitimate form of compassion toward personal beliefs that a secular society can offer.

Ultimate Reality, Provable Reality, Secular Neutrality

As I close, I want to speak about two different realities: one, an absolute, ultimate one; and the other, a pragmatic, provable one. As I said before, I am a religious man. God, prophets, angels, scriptures, revelation—I believe in these things and more. Yet, none of that is provable, not in a secular sense, so how is it that a person like me who believes such things can, on the other hand, speak so much about proof and argue that our society's reality must be determined by proof?

The answer is that I'm not speaking here as a member of my religion. I have beliefs about reality, about an absolute, ultimate reality, and make no mistake—I am no relativist: I believe that I am *right.* But there are eight billion other humans on this planet, and most of them likely believe they are right as well. So how are we going to live together? We have to have some common ground—a common *reality*—so that we can interact together, build communities, and form laws to protect our rights. But whose vision of ultimate reality should we use?

Well, given that I am right, the answer is obvious: everyone should use mine. Unfortunately, some of the eight billion other humans disagree, so what shall we do? History provides countless examples of one solution: We could go to war. We could war and we could war until one of us emerges the stronger and imposes their vision of ultimate reality on everyone else through force. Then, after they lose their power, we could war again and again, repeating the cycle endlessly.

But recent centuries have provided a different option. Through the Enlightenment and the scientific revolution there came a realization that Nature itself has a voice if we're willing to listen. This is the voice of proof, of scientific observation. It is a limited voice. It knows nothing about morality or the meaning of life, and ultimate reality itself remains elusive to it. But the voice of Nature is sufficient to provide a new vision of reality: a provable reality. Now, in comparison to our personal vision of ultimate reality this isn't the *real* reality, but it's a pragmatic one. It's sufficient for its purpose. Because now, for the first time, we have an alternate option instead of constantly warring over who gets to decide what reality is. Now we can all agree to let Nature decide for us, to let the proof provide a shared reality for us and thereby stop the never-ending wars.

This is the concept of secular neutrality: a common

ground based entirely on proof that we can build our society upon. Yet secular neutrality is only a bare foundation for society. It cannot provide everything we need to live our lives. It doesn't contain morality, virtue, or honor. It doesn't explain the meaning of life. It doesn't reveal the nature of ultimate reality. Those things can only come through our personal vision of ultimate reality, which means we need some way to combine the two, to allow provable reality to set the foundation for our society—its laws, its governance—and yet still allow us to live based on our own personal vision of ultimate reality.

The solution is religious freedom. We all bundle our beliefs about ultimate reality into religions, allowing us to be granted space to live according to our beliefs, while not infringing on the right of others to live according to their own religions. It is not perfect, but I believe that a society founded on secular neutrality with robust religious freedom is the most just arrangement possible for us.

So I'm not speaking to you here as a member of my religion. I'm speaking to you as a secular citizen. And, as a secular citizen, I'm trying to persuade you to see the value in secular neutrality and to understand that the LGBT movement is violating it. Secular neutrality is a truce. The LGBT movement is breaking that truce. Our core beliefs about ultimate reality are supposed to be claimed as religious, thereby making clear what is part of secular neutrality and what is not, but they have refused to do this, preferring instead to exploit a weakness in our current laws: We haven't yet learned how to protect ourselves from a religion that refuses to call itself a religion.

And so, yes, I am a religious man yet I am using the language of secularism because I understand the nature of the fight we are in and I see secularism as our friend in this fight, not our foe. I am fighting for secular neutrality. It is being threatened today, perhaps more than it has ever been threatened before. I hope you will join me.

Summary

There is no valid proof of gender identity, and based on the current fields of science there never will be. Reality cannot be determined based on claims of happiness because one person's happiness conflicts with another's and because human emotions aren't a reliable way to determine it. Reality also cannot be determined based on claims of identity because identity is just a personal belief and one person's identity conflicts with another's. Nothing based on self-identity can be considered immutable because we have no way to *know* what the value is and hence cannot know if it has changed. And it is unjust for psychologists to expect people to affirm the personal beliefs of their patients. The universe does not revolve around their patients. Other people matter too, and we have the right to not treat unprovable beliefs as true.

Using brain scans to "prove" gender identity, while never allowing them to disprove it, is an example of religious apologetics, not science. The only way for a secular society to provide compassion for personal beliefs is through religious freedom. If people choose to not take that route, then that is their choice, but they will have to accept the consequences because secular neutrality *must* be protected. Under no circumstances can a secular society treat gender identity, or anything based on self-identity, as true.

Appendix: Original Publication Dates

- The Coming Out
  - July 8, 2021
- The Freedom to Not Believe
  - July 17, 2021
- Gender Identity and the Invisible Pasta God
  - August 22, 2018
- There Can Be No Demigods in Secularism
  - March 24, 2022
- Unwanted Proof
  - July 13, 2019
- It's Gender-Obscuring, Not Gender-Affirming
  - August 18, 2022
- A Principal's Conundrum
  - August 5, 2021
- What is a Woman? Answered
  - September 7, 2022

- The Psychologist
  - August 18, 2021
- Provable Reality, Cold and Indifferent
  - February 17, 2023
- Converting the Two-Spirit
  - September 22, 2021
- There Is No Valid Proof of Gender Identity, And There Never Will Be
  - March 25, 2023

stephenmeasure.com

www.ingramcontent.com/pod-product-compliance
Lightning Source LLC
LaVergne TN
LVHW090942080826
845145LV00003B/857

* 9 7 8 1 9 4 0 7 7 8 5 3 2 *